FINDING

LOVE AGAIN

Crystal Lake, Montana

By: Christa Ann

Finding Love Again
Crystal Lake, Montana – Book 1

© Copyright 2016 Christa Ann

Published by After Glows
PO Box 224
Middleburg, Fl. 32050

Digital ISBN: 978-1-944060-12-1
Print ISBN: 978-1-944060-13-8

Cover by
Formatting by AG Formatting

AfterGlowsPublishing.com

DEDICATIONS

To my husband who put up with me staying up late during the week and up even later during the weekend. But mostly for his love and support.

To Lia Davis who is not only a fantastic author put a great person and friend. Thank you for all your help and support. And for answering all my endless questions.

FINDING LOVE AGAIN

Widow Shannon Ward lives for her job and her children. Her closed off heart helps her hide from the pain of losing her husband suddenly. Her four best friends and children decide she needs to get out and live again. A 'girls only' vacation to the Mountains of Montana might be just what she needs. Finding love again is farthest from her mind and definitely not on her to-do list. However, a certain sexy rancher could change her mind...

Rancher Ryan Collins finally divorced his high school sweetheart. The only good thing that came out of the marriage were his three children. Ryan is done with love and women. He's happy with running his ranch and being a bachelor...or so he thinks until he meets Shannon.

Two hearts closed off from love and determined to stay that way, until that first glance. Will Shannon and Ryan risk their hearts one more time or just walk away?

ONE

Although the view might be stunning to some, all Shannon could see were wide open spaces of nothingness. The land was green, sure, but so was mold. Frustration bubbled in her stomach, and she couldn't help blurting out for the fourth time, "I can't believe I let you three talk me into this. What was I thinking? Tell me again, why you decided I should leave Florida? We didn't have to come out West for a vacation. We could've just gone to the Keys or even St. Augustine."

Lisa, her best friend, glared at her in the rearview mirror. "Here we go again. Damn it, Shannon, you had five weeks of vacation. You deserve some time off. I know you miss your husband, but he wouldn't want you to be sitting around while life passes you by. He would want you to live and maybe find love again."

Shannon glanced away from her friend. Lisa would know. She'd met Tom in college and they'd become good friends. The two of them had had a lot of discussions about life. But when they'd started talking about leaving family behind in the event of death, Shannon would leave the room. The thought of not having Tom with her and the children made her sick to her stomach. Shannon never thought she would have to face that situation.

Lisa could be a pain in the ass sometimes, but she meant well. She just didn't understand. *I loved my husband. He meant everything to me.* After the car accident that took Tom's life, Shannon just didn't have the energy to go anywhere. However, her so-called friends, along with her loving children, talked her into going to the mountains for two weeks. The first 'girls only' vacation, they called it. Every year, going forward, they planned to go somewhere different.

As they drove through the small town of Crystal Lake, Montana, the beauty of the mountains along with the clear blue sky relaxed Shannon both in body and mind. The slight chill to the air made it too cool for shorts and t-shirts, but warm enough not to need a coat. She could breathe better without all the fumes from cars, and the only sounds were birds, not people yelling or horns from cars. A soft touch on Shannon's shoulder alerted her that Bianca wanted to lend her support. Always the peacemaker, wanting to comfort when needed or smooth high emotions.

With the sun shining in through the open window Bianca's soft brown hair flowed up around her head giving her an angelic look. "This is going to be fun! We all needed a vacation away. I read somewhere that there is a ranch where you can go horseback riding. You told us that when you lived in Maryland, you had horses. There's a resort that's popular in the winter for their skiing. We can go there and check it out."

With her signature contagious smile, Erica beamed at Shannon, and she couldn't help but grin back. "Horseback riding would be fantastic. I'm hoping we could all go hiking and take pictures of the scenery."

"Oh, for the love of God! Will you stop being Mary Sunshine, Bibi?" Lisa said, using Bianca's nickname—teasing based on the look on her face, which made Bianca and Shannon dissolve into laughter.

"Why don't we find someplace to eat before we head to the cabin? We had a long flight and we didn't get a chance to have any lunch, so we can have an early dinner." Shannon smiled. *Okay, vacation starts now.*

Lisa didn't wait for anyone to answer. Instead, she just pulled into a parking space on Main Street. Shannon got out of the SUV, needing to stretched the soreness from her legs, arms, and back and noticed a park two blocks away. Couples held hands and families played with their children, all enjoying the beauty of day. They'd parked about a block from Frank's Diner. Shannon looked across the street at a store called "A Little Bit of Everything." As they headed to the diner, everyone smiled and some said "hello" or "evening." Before opening the door to the diner, another sign caught Shannon's eye: "Conway Books." *Yes, a bookstore!*

A little bell jingled as they opened the door to the diner. The smell of bread and apple pie hit Shannon's nose and her stomach growled. She instantly recognized home cooking. A woman behind the counter, wearing a colorful plaid apron, looked up and hollered, "Just take seat anywhere. I'll be with you folks in a minute."

Only three places were available, two tables and one booth. They took the round table in the back corner so they could see everything. The place appeared very busy, so the food must be fantastic. Everyone talked and said hello to their group as they made their way to the table. The waitress came over with menus and a smile. She wore jeans with a light blue t-shirt that said *Frank's Diner* in white letters and a nametag that read 'Nell'. "You ladies aren't from around here, are ya? Where are you from?"

"We're on vacation from Florida," Lisa replied.

"Are you planning on staying or just passing through? The county fair is in a couple of days. There'll be some crafts, cakes and pies up for sale, along with the best barbeque you'll find in the county. Some of the boys and girls from the high school will be singing. There will be other events going on: a contest with the local livestock and a bakery contest, too. It's a lot of fun." Nell's words bubbled with obvious excitement and her grin never wavered. She clearly looked forward to the fair and loved her town.

"Well, we'll definitely be here. We're renting a cabin from Mr. Lawson for two weeks. I just hope it gets a little warmer." Erica smiled.

"Oh, don't you worry about that. You'll be wearing shorts and t-shirts by then. In the meanwhile, what can I get you to drink? Oh, I nearly forgot to tell you about the special. The special for today is steak, mashed potatoes with gravy, broccoli, salad, and a slice of apple pie. You can replace the pie with one of the other desserts, if you'd like." Nell pulled a pad and pen from the pocket of her apron and prepared to write down their orders.

Lisa ordered a soda, as if she needed any more caffeine. Bianca got water with lemon, Erica and Shannon ordered sweet tea. Nell went off the get their drinks while they looked over the menu. Everything looked so good that Shannon struggled to decide what she wanted.

Nell returned with their drinks and a basket of warm rolls. "Do you know what you'd like or do you need a minute?"

Shannon, Lisa, and Erica ordered the special. Bianca had to be the odd one out and ordered a chicken salad — she was on another of her diets. Bianca worked in a bakery and thought of herself as overweight. Shannon would love to have some of Bianca's curves. Nell went off to put their order in and promised to come back in a few minutes to refill their drinks.

Shannon got out her cell phone and took a quick look at Lisa and Bianca. "I really need to call Dylan and Alexis to let them know we got here okay. I don't want them to worry. I'm just going to step outside; it's just too loud in here. If the food gets here before I get back, come and get me."

"Okay. But don't be long. We're on vacation." Lisa looked up after texting her boyfriend, Brad, that she had arrived safely.

"Tell them we said hello and will talk to them later." Erica just put her phone away from letting her parents know they'd arrived and adjusted her blond hair with her red headband. Bianca was already typing a text to her brother, who had her three-year-old daughter, Mia.

Shannon called her son first, because Dylan would be a fast call. Being in the Army, he wouldn't be able to stay on the phone long. He might not be able to answer the phone, so she likely would have to leave a message. *Please let me just leave a message.*

"Hi, Mom. Did you get there okay? Everything okay with the rental and the drive to the cabin? You four didn't have any problems, right?" Dylan shot off the questions before Shannon could answer him.

"Yes, dear. I arrived here okay. Everything went fine with getting the rental, and Lisa drove like a madwoman down the highway. We're having dinner before going to the cabin.

Is there anything else you'd like to know?" Shannon just had to add that last part. She knew her son worried, and she loved him for that.

He started to laugh. "Okay, okay. I got it. However, everything good? If you and your friends need anything, just give me a call. I'll get there or get you help. If I can get some time off, I'll come out there to see you. Would that be alright with everyone else?"

"It'd be great if you could come and see everyone. It's been almost nine months since I've seen you. I'll call you later, alright?"

"Okay, Mom. Please tell everyone I said hello and let Ms. Lisa know to stay out of trouble. I hope that I can see you soon. I gotta go, Mom. I have guard duty tonight."

"Love you. Be careful and safe." Shannon had to smile when she hung up the phone. God, she loved her son. He would do anything for anyone, just like his father. Calm in a crisis, he listened to the problem, analyzed it, and came up with a solution.

Now, for the hard phone call—her daughter. *God, give me strength.*

"Mom! It's about time you called. Where have you been? Your flight landed four hours ago. What took you so long to call me? Did something go wrong? Are you okay? Do you need me to come and get you? Did you have a hard time with the rental? Oh, my God, did it break down? Did some..." Alexis rambled on faster than her brother had.

"Alexis, stop!" Shannon loved her, but she worried more than Dylan.

"Well?" Alexis questioned.

"Everything is okay — the flight and the rental. And, no, the SUV didn't break down. We're having dinner before going to the cabin. You need to stop worrying. I'm the parent here, and forty-five years old. I think I can take care of myself," Shannon answered her daughter with a smile on her face. Her daughter was more like her than she wanted to admit. She loved with all her heart and would do anything for the people who meant the most to her without question or reservation. But, like Shannon, she didn't like family to fight or see them hurt.

"I'm just worried. This is your first vacation since Dad died. Well, shit, I shouldn't have said that. Sorry." The hurt resonated in Alexis' voice.

Shannon's vision blurred from the sorrow in her daughter's voice. Placing a hand below her neck to keep the lump in her throat from preventing her to speak, she said, "Yes, it is my first big trip, but, I think your dad wouldn't want me sitting around the house anymore." She practically quoted what she'd just heard from one of her dearest friends. "Your father's death hit us all hard, but it's time for me to try to get out and live life."

"When you didn't call, I got worried that someone hit the rental. Just like Dad. I know it's dumb to jump to that conclusion, but I just couldn't seem to stop thinking about it. The drunk driver, the phone call from the police, and then the ride to the hospital, only to be too late… I'm sorry I jumped on you that way, but when you were late calling..." Alexis stopped to sigh deeply.

"It's okay. I'll talk to you later. I promise to call. Okay?" Shannon just wanted her daughter to be happy for her and to get off the phone. She really loved her, but she didn't want to drudge up bad memories on her vacation.

"Okay, Mom. Just call me later and, please, please be careful and safe. I don't want to lose you, too." Alexis might be a whirlwind, but she had good intentions.

"I will." As Shannon hung up the phone, the back of her eyes started to burn. She blinked fast in order to stop from crying. She loved her children with all her heart and soul.

They'd always been close, but since Tom passed away they'd become even closer. They even tried to get her to move closer to one of them. She sat outside for a little while to get herself together. She didn't want to worry her friends. *I need this vacation to start living again. We all deserve to be happy again. But can I ever replace the one man who had my heart?*

* * *

Ryan watched Hank, his foreman, exercise the new horse that arrived the day before—Argo, a dark brown Quarter Horse with a black mane.

"Hey, Dad!" Dustin yelled.

"Hey, son. What took you so long to find me? Did you decide to take the day off or something?" Ryan tilted his black Stetson up to look at his oldest son—well, the oldest of his twin boys. He looked so much like his mother with his black hair, brown eyes, and his olive skin tone, though he got his height from Ryan, standing six-foot to his six-two. "What do you think? He's a beaut."

"I came to tell you Steve is coming down the road." Dustin turned to the new animal. "He's going to be a good addition, and the ladies are going to love him, just like Thunder."

Ryan, Steve, and JP had been friends since first grade. Went to school together, played football together, and did just about everything together. They'd become something more like brothers than best friends. Frank, who owned the diner in town, became their fourth when his family moved to Crystal Lake during middle school. The four of them were hell on wheels and they only got worse in high school. *Damn, what a long time ago,* Ryan thought to himself.

"Okay. I'll run up to the house to see what's up," Ryan commented over his shoulder as he headed that direction. He didn't have to worry about the ranch between Hank and his two sons, as they all knew what needed to be done.

"Take your time. Hank and I got everything covered here," Dustin responded.

Ryan noticed Steve waiting for him by his black Chevy Silverado. "Hey, old man. What the hell is going on?"

Ryan shook his head and held out his hand to shake. "Not much. Lose the old man bullshit. You're the same age as me, dumb ass. You don't have something better to do than bother me? Shouldn't you be waiting for whoever you rented the cabin to?"

"Nah. I told them that the cabin would be

unlocked and the keys hanging on the hook by the door. I'll go by tomorrow sometime just to introduce myself. Want to go have an early dinner?"

Ryan stood there and stared at this best friend. *He must think I'm stupid.* "Bullshit. One of my sons called you. Which one, Dustin or Colby? Had to have been Dustin. That damn boy needs to mind his own fucking business."

"Look, your sons and I noticed you haven't done a damn thing outside of your ranch. The divorce was finalized three years ago, and your sorry ass hasn't been out since. So let's go and do something, man. Your sons have the ranch; your daughter will be fine when she gets off from work. We'll go have an early dinner at the diner then go to *After Hours* for some beer. Maybe some two-stepping with some of the single women, just like old times. Unless you're too old for some fun…" His ornery grin tempted Ryan to agree. Steve could give anyone that grin and get exactly what he wanted; you just couldn't deny him. His whole face lit up with excitement.

Their friend, JP, inherited the ranch during their senior year of high school after his parents passed way, and then opened *After Hours*. He hated ranch life and planned to move, but with some advice from his friends, along with his cousin Nell, they'd converted the Equestrian into *After Hours*. It became a place where anyone could come and hang out, drink, listen to music, and dance up a storm. He hadn't been to After Hours in years, because Vicky — his ex-wife — hated the place. Frank, Steve, and Ryan used to go to *After Hours* and hang out, drink beer, and dance with all the single girls.

Ryan noticed that Steve only mentioned his sons and not his daughter. He worried that she still believed that her parents might get back together. "Alright, just let me tell my good for nothing sons I'm outta here."

"I know I can do everything right, so you must be talking about Dustin." Colby, Dustin's twin, came out of the house in sweatpants and a t-shirt. He looked the most like his father. Brown hair with blue gray eyes and even six-one. At twenty-three, he had a body of a running back.

"Are you eating again? Or have you been out running?" asked Ryan.

"Came in to get some sandwiches and iced tea. I got mud all over my jeans when I was fixing the fence out on the south ridge. Didn't want to track it all over the kitchen because Rosa would have my ass." Colby did not want to make the housekeeper mad. The last time that happened, he didn't have clean clothes for a week, and she wouldn't make his favorite cookies.

"Steve and I are going to the diner to eat and might stop afterward at *After Hours*. Call me on my cell if the three of you need anything. Your sister is working until five. It would be nice of the two of you to eat dinner with her before you go to your place." His two sons moved into the original cabin on the property that Ryan and his sister, Rena, grew up in. It gave them the space they needed while keeping them close. Then again, they still ate dinner at the main house and left their dirty laundry in the basket for the housekeeper. Neither one wanted Rosa in their cabin to clean or collect laundry. They were too afraid she'd show up when they had company — the female kind. He didn't understand it really, as only Colby had a girlfriend as far as he knew. Still, he had a feeling that the three of them were up to something. Ryan knew of some couples involved in ménage relationships. He didn't judge, not as long as no one forced them or got hurt. The ménage relationships he knew of are very happy. Not seeing Dustin with anyone made him wonder.

"We got it. See you sometime in the morning." Colby jogged back to the house, trying his best not to laugh.

"Everyone knows, so let's leave. I'm getting hungry." Steve opened the driver's side door and started up his truck. Ryan hopped into the passenger side and, before he got the door completely closed, Steve had already started to drive down the road to the highway. *The crazy bastard.*

TWO

When Shannon reentered the diner, she noticed Nell had started to deliver their salads. She took her seat next to Bianca as she said, "Just in time. We thought we'd have to come out to get you."

Lisa looked up from her phone. "So how are Dylan and Alexis? Everything go okay?"

"Yeah, everything is good. I should have called them when we landed. Alexis worried that we might have gotten into an accident. I felt bad," Shannon replied. Lisa drove Shannon to the hospital when she'd gotten the call from the police about her husband.

Erica joked about Shannon needing to be wrapped in bubble wrap when the bell on the door jingled. They all glanced up and Shannon fell into the most beautiful blue-gray eyes she had ever seen. Butterflies fluttered in her stomach and the palms of her hands started to get clammy. *Oh my God, what is wrong with me?*

Erica leaned over and whispered to Nell, loud enough for them all to hear her, "Who are those two handsome men?"

"Oh, that's Ryan Collins and Steve Lawson."

"Married or single?" Lisa asked with a grin.

Erica stabbed her fork into a cucumber before pondering out loud, "We're renting the cabin from Mr. Lawson. I wonder if it's the same man."

"Steve does rent out four cabins. In addition, to answer your question, Steve has never been married. Ryan's divorce has been final for about three years now, thank goodness. His ex-wife is a real bitch. He has twin sons and one daughter. His sons work the ranch and his daughter helps out over at the bookstore," Nell whispered.

Shannon just couldn't keep her eyes off the man with the gorgeous eyes.

Nell called out, "Ryan, Steve, come on over here a minute."

As he made his way over, Shannon couldn't help but notice how his blue jeans hugged him in all the right places, as did his blue and white flannel shirt. His chest and biceps stretched the fabric of his shirt in a way that made Shannon think it might rip apart. Brown hair showed under his black Stetson. His square jawline was darkened with a slight five o'clock shadow. As she moved her eyes upward, she again got lost in his gorgeous eyes. Everything started to fade away as she looked deeper into those eyes.

At the light tap on her knee, Shannon cleared her throat. Her mouth had gone dry, and she wiped her hands on her jeans. Lisa leaned over. "Shannon, you doing okay? You look a little flushed. Something or someone getting to you?" Her smirk gave away the fact that she knew what bothered her.

Shannon kicked her friend under the table and gave her a look that told her to shut up. She started to open her month when the two cowboys stopped next to Nell. *Oh shit, what did Nell say their names are again? He's much taller close up and… those eyes.*

* * *

Ryan and Steve opened the door to the diner and scanned for an open table. *The place is busy.* Glancing around, he saw Nell talking to four ladies at the round table in the back. As soon as Ryan noticed a pair of big blue eyes that reminded him of the sky, Nell called them over. Steven said, "Looks like Nell needs us. Maybe we have four ladies to entertain."

"I only want to talk to the one with those beautiful sky-blue eyes." Ryan hastily glanced at Steve and realized he'd said that thought out loud. "Forget I said that. You didn't hear anything."

Steve stared at Ryan in shock. "So, you want to get to know the one with the blue eyes and brown curly hair? Let's go over and see what we can find out."

"Steve, now don't you..." Ryan began before Steve rushed over to Nell. He wanted to get the hell out of there before Steve made an ass of not only him, but Ryan, too. *What am I thinking? I don't need the complications of another woman in my life.*

By the time Ryan got to the table, Nell already introduced everyone. Steve talked to the ladies when they realized that he owned the cabin they were renting. Ryan didn't want to be there. He just wanted to eat dinner, go home — after he kicked Steve's ass.

Nell turned to Ryan. "I just introduced the girls to Steve. This is Lisa, Erica, Bianca, and Shannon. They're on vacation from Florida."

Ryan just shrugged. "That's great. Nell, can we have two specials? We'll go take one of the vacant tables."

"Oh, you and Steve can sit with us. We'll be happy to make room," Lisa offered with a big smile. *Oh, she's just as bad as Steve.*

"That'd be great, thank you." Steve answered Lisa faster than Ryan. He planned to seriously kick his friend's ass.

Ryan and Steve grabbed chairs to join them. Lisa got up and shifted to allow one of them to sit by Shannon. Steve took the seat by Lisa, which left Ryan the seat by Shannon. As Ryan sat down, his knee rubbed up against Shannon's. "Um, sorry," Ryan muttered.

The conversation continued around the table, but Ryan didn't hear everything being said. He found himself too engrossed with the woman sitting next to him. They were close enough that he could smell the teasing scent of her — coconuts. It reminded him of coconuts. He wondered if was from her shampoo or body wash. Shannon didn't meet his occasional glances her direction. Nell delivered everyone's dinner. As the group ate and chatted, Steve asked Shannon a question.

"Did I miss something?" The red flushing her cheeks let Ryan know he caught her off guard.

"Lisa just mentioned that you have a son in

the Army. I asked where he's stationed and what he did." Steven could only smile, knowing that Shannon kept looking at Ryan.

"Oh, my son Dylan is stationed in Colorado. He's in Special Forces. He plans to make it a career. My daughter Alexis goes to college and works as a photographer part time. She lives in Maryland near my parents." She paused, face flushing even redder, then blurted, "Bibi has a three-year-old daughter name Mia." Shannon obviously wanted to get the attention away from her and on someone else.

"We should all go to *After Hours*. Our friend, JP, owns the place. We can have a drink and dance. Right, Ryan?"

Ryan plotted to throw his friend off the damn mountain.

"Only if you're up to it." What else could Ryan say.

"I'm not sure. We had a long flight and it drained a lot of my energy," Shannon said shyly.

Dessert arrived, delivered by the owner, Frank—three slices of apple pie and one of blueberry pie. Everything tasted absolutely delicious and Ryan could tell that Shannon started to relax. *Food tends to do that.*

"You know, Frank, Bianca works in a bakery, and she makes the best key lime pie. You should try to convince her to make one before we leave." Lisa spared the owner of the diner a sly grin.

Ryan decided he should let her know that Frank and Nell were together before she caused offense with her overt matchmaking.

Frank turned to Bianca. "I would love for you to make something. I'm always looking for new recipes for the diner, if it's not too much trouble."

"Oh, sure, if I have time," Bianca replied. Her blush was charming, but her knuckles whitened on the table, relaying her distress. Ryan glanced at Steve, and they both knew something was not quite right.

They agreed to have the girls follow Steve to the cabin. Fifteen minutes later, they arrived. They planned to give them some time to settle in then meet up at the cabin at nine to go to *After Hours*.

Ryan knew that all the cabins were gorgeous. Two bedrooms with full bathrooms attached, kitchen with modern applications, living room with a stone fireplace and television/Blu-ray player on a stand across from the sofa and love seat. The cabin the ladies had rented also had hardwood floors with area rugs everywhere. Steve stocked the kitchen previously with any basic things his renters might need for their stay.

"I got that. Where do you want it?" Ryan asked Shannon as he carried in two suitcases.

Shannon followed Ryan down the hall. "That's mine and Lisa's. So, one goes in each room. Thank you for carrying them." Turning around, she added, "Bianca, we're in the room on the right. Lisa and Erica will be on the left."

"Not a problem." Ryan could only stare into her blue eyes. They reminded him of the sky on a clear day. "You have the bluest eyes that I've ever seen." *Shit, did I say that out loud?*

Ducking his head, he could see the slight blush on her cheeks. "Thank you."

They headed back into the kitchen and heard Steve's last sentence. "So, we will be back here at nine o'clock. That enough time for everyone to freshen up?"

"Good with us," Erica answered.

Turning, he said to Shannon, "I guess we'll see you at nine." He rushed for the door and Steve's truck. His friend, soon to be ex-friend, would be getting an earful. *Maybe.*

* * *

As they headed back to the cabin to meet

up with the ladies so they could follow them to *After Hours*, Ryan watched the scenery pass by. The sky was so clear that he could see the stars for miles and the mountain guarding the town. "So," Steve began and Ryan looked at his friend. *Oh man, here we go.* "What do you think?"

"About what?" Ryan knew he sounded irritated.

Steve just rolled his eyes, "About the sky. What do you think I'm talking about, dumb ass?"

Steve could be like a dog with a bone. He wouldn't give up until Ryan answered his damn question. The thing was, it really wasn't a question — more like a statement — but Ryan knew what he referred to. *Shannon.* He didn't want to go there. So, he said the only thing he knew to say. "I don't know."

"Okay, you're telling me you didn't notice any of them? I'm not that stupid, man. Come on. You looked at Shannon like she was a damn ice cream cone you wanted to lick, and she snuck looks at you. I thought the two of you were going to jump each other at the diner, what with all the heat between you two. Tell me I'm wrong?" Steve had a smile on his face that Ryan wanted to smack.

Then it hit Ryan. She'd looked at him.

Why? He didn't notice. "Are you sure? I mean, not that I care or anything. Shit, I sound like fucking idiot." Ryan rested his head on the headrest.

"Well, you can ask her to dance at *After Hours*. I'm going to ask Lisa or maybe Erica." Steve smiled at him.

"What's wrong with Bianca?" Ryan asked.

Steve just shrugged. "Nothing. But, she's a little quiet and shy. Not really my type."

Ryan raised his head as they pulled up to the cabin. He wanted to sit with Shannon and get to know her. Just listen to her voice. *What does she like?* Did she like sitting outside and watching the rain, or sitting on couch with a blanket in front of the fireplace when it got cold? Would she want to go horseback riding and eat lunch by the lake? What were her dreams? Ryan felt like a teenager going up to the front door to pick up his first date.

The front door opened and Erica let Ryan and Steve inside. "We're in the living room, relaxing and waiting for the damn party to start."

Ryan couldn't take his eyes off Shannon. She wore blue jeans, a light blue blouse with flowers outlined in black, and black boots. She'd pulled her hair back in a turquoise clip and wore very little makeup. Steve was the first one to find his voice. "You ladies all ready to go?"

As they left the cabin, Ryan hung back to wait for Shannon. "You look beautiful, Shannon. Save a dance for me? I didn't think to ask if you two-step."

"Yes. I mean thank you and, yes, I'll save you a dance," Shannon answered.

THREE

They got to *After Hours* in about twenty-five minutes. It looked like an equestrian building. Shannon stopped to get a better look at the building and Ryan stopped with her. "Is there a problem?"

"Oh, no. It's just the building looks like..."

Ryan finished her sentence. "An equestrian building. Yes, it is or rather, it was. JP's parents passed away, but he really didn't like ranching. So he remodeled the building into *After Hours*. The barn has been changed into storage for the bar and other extra equipment. He worked hard to make this a place that the community would want to have. Now, we don't have to drive to the next town — almost two hours away — to have a beer and dance. We come here. How do you know about equestrian buildings?"

Ryan and Shannon headed into the building while she told him, "I grew up in Maryland and had horses. My parents boarded them at an equestrian center. I used to go there every chance I got. I don't get a chance to ride much anymore, though. I miss having my own horse."

"I have ten horses now and some cattle. I prefer horses. Venus is pregnant and due any day. She's a cross between a Tennessee Walker and Quarter Horse, and she's expecting twins." Ryan loved his horses. "Do you ride western or English style?"

"Western, of course." Shannon said it in a way that suggested the question was stupid. Well, maybe it was. Ryan found himself very impressed that she knew so much about horses. They had a lot more in common than he'd guessed.

Entering from the side, they noticed the place was already crowded. In the back left corner, a mechanical bull stood proudly, and on the back right side, two pool tables were set up alongside two dartboards. The bar on the right side had stools lined up and racks behind it filled with glasses and all kinds of liquor. Table and chairs lined the front and on the other side, which left the middle for the dancers. However, the front right corner boasted a riser for a band to set up and play.

A stereo system was wired with speakers attached to all four corners of the building. The bar had a main unit that controlled the music.

Two very tall, large men stalked around the tables and, boy, they looked alike. "The bouncers are Max and Mitch. If you couldn't tell, they're identical twins," Ryan told Shannon.

Ryan noticed Shannon scanning everywhere as they approached one of the larger tables, and knew what she was searching for. "There's a hallway between the pool tables and the bar that leads to the restrooms. JP had to add them to the building." He looked down at her while he pulled out her chair.

"Thank you for letting me know. He definitely has a lot of different things here. Does he have a live band every night?" Shannon's smile lit up the room.

Before Ryan could answer, a waitress by the name of Stacy came over with two bowls: pretzels and peanuts. They all ordered beers. Steve asked her to let JP know that they'd arrived when she had a chance. Frank and Nell planned to join them once they closed the diner.

"No, he doesn't always have a band here.

That's why he installed a stereo system. But, he does try. Most of the bands are locals, no one famous or anything. Those two are bouncers, and they try to keep it peaceful. They're also JP's cousins. The waitress you met today at Frank's Diner, Nell, is also JP's cousin and she's dating Frank. She helps out here when one of the waitresses gets sick and the other girls can't come in to help," Ryan explained.

The music played. The two pool tables stayed busy and, every once in a while, the bull gave a cowboy the ride of his life. Steve told the ladies that the bull didn't run all night. JP had set times and a sign-up sheet, so everyone knew who rode next and at what time. JP worked hard to keep the bar organized.

When "You Look Good in My Shirt" by Keith Urban came on, Ryan ask Shannon to dance with him. Steve asked if one of the other three ladies would like to dance with him at the same time. Erica jumped at the chance to go for a spin around the dance floor. Ryan and Shannon continued to dance when the song ended. Every time Shannon stepped on Ryan's foot, they would both start laughing. After "Rain Is a Good Thing" by Luke Bryan, they went back to the table to sit, talk, and enjoy everyone's company.

JP stopped by to see Ryan and Steve, and they introduced everyone. His cousins made a round or two, but they mostly talked to Bianca. Everyone had a great time, meeting members of the town and dancing. Ryan saved every dance for Shannon and had the time of his life. He only had one thought going through his mind. *I shouldn't enjoy being with Shannon.*

At about twelve-thirty in the morning, Shannon and her friends decided to leave. Ryan and Steve walked them out to their car.

Shannon turned to Ryan. "Thank you for inviting us. We had a great time."

"I'm glad you all came. You should come to the ranch and go riding. We can take the horses to the lake, have a picnic lunch, and go swimming. You and your friends, I mean," Ryan added.

Wanting to say yes right away, Shannon responded instead, "I'll let you know."

He watched Shannon and her friends leave, then Ryan left with Steve to head home.

* * *

She needed to really think about whether or not she wanted to see him again. Why would she get involved with someone who lived so far away? Could she have just a summer fling and not let her heart get involved? She just wasn't sure.

On the way back to the cabin, her friends talked about everything that had happened and the people they'd met. "Did you notice how nice the people here are, unlike back home. In Florida, they avoid looking at you. Everyone knows everyone else here and asks about family and their businesses."

Shannon thought about how much she had in common with Ryan. He was just so easy to talk to, and his sense of humor… What shocked her the most was that she had fun with him. Even during her marriage with Tom, there were times that they had nothing to say or just had no interest in what the other one did.

Lisa interrupted her thinking. "You and Ryan did a lot of talking. Did you two have fun?"

"We talked about his horses, his ranch, and possibly going horseback riding and having a picnic at the lake. What do you guys think?" Shannon asked them with a slight blush.

"I don't know about you two, but I bet that Ryan really only wanted to ask Shannon and not all of us. I think he wanted to have some alone time. So he can really get to know our Shannon without so many people around."

Erika sounded like she was only kidding, but Shannon wasn't too sure.

Shannon looked at one of her closest friends with annoyance. "He's just being nice, and friendly."

"Oh, sure he is, honey. Bianca, Erika, and I can just see it now. All four of us, Ryan and maybe Steve, riding under the moonlight and then relaxing by the lake under the stars. How are four ladies going to make out with two guys?" Lisa started laughing hysterically.

"He said lunchtime, you idiot, not dinner. So, no moonlight, stars, or swimming naked."

"Hey, I never said anything about swimming naked. But that would be damn fun—to see Ryan and Steve strolling from the lake, naked, with all their muscles shining in the moonlight. The water running down from their hair to their necks and chests. Then traveling down to six-pack abs and navel. Then down even further to…."

"That's enough, Lisa. I've heard just about enough." Only Lisa would say something like that. Well, Erika would, too. Shannon know exactly where she would go next, and she didn't want to hear any more.

That's when Erika just had to chime in with, "…their cocks!" Bianca blushed and

Shannon just shook her head. "Had to go there. Sorry. Well, I'm not really sorry."

"I'm going to bed now. See you all in the morning." Shannon might not be able to sleep, now that Lisa had planted that image of Ryan emerging from the lake naked and wet. Water running down his body from those wide shoulders, over that massive chest, to his ripped six-pack abs down to his hard…. *Stop, just stop. Now I need a cold damn shower.*

As Shannon went down the hall to the room she shared with Bianca, she could hear Lisa and Erika laughing their fool heads off. *Great, just great.*

FOUR

The next two days went by faster than anyone wanted. They went shopping at some of the local stores and did a lot of hiking trails. Shannon and Erika both brought their cameras so they would have a lot of pictures. The scenery was gorgeous.

The top of the mountains still had some snow on them. Mule deer and Pronghorn sheep were everywhere, feeding with their young. The even got to see the state bird, the Western Meadowlark—yellow along the chest and underneath they had a black "V" on their chest. The back was white with streaks of black, and their heads were streaked with brown, white with very little yellow.

That morning, they ate breakfast at the cabin and discussed the county fair, which began that day. None of them had ever attended a county fair before. While they talked, Shannon looked at her camera to make sure that all her pictures came out okay from the hike yesterday.

"Hey, Lisa, do you think Ryan will be at the fair?" *Oh, Erica started early this morning.* When they'd went to town to eat at the diner, she'd asked Nell if she had seen Ryan.

Picking up her coffee, Lisa answered, "Oh, I bet he will be. Nell said yesterday that everyone will be there. He'll be looking for Shannon."

"Both of you need to shut the hell up." Shannon threw a piece of toast at Lisa. "I'm not getting involved with someone else. Besides, if I wanted to date I would date someone back home. Why would I get involved with him?" Shannon looked at all three of them.

"Well, let's get going. I want to see everything." Erica picked up her purse and started toward the door after placing her breakfast dishes in the dishwasher.

They headed out the door and drove toward the park, which sat three blocks from the diner. They lucked out, finding a parking space one block from the fair. It looked like all the stores were closed so that everyone could attend.

On one side of the grounds, games lined up—things like ring toss, water guns to blow up balloons, and bottle bust. Two games of horseshoes were going on and the men playing were almost as loud as the kids running around laughing. The prizes ranged from stuffed animals to discounts at some of the stores, or even coupons for the diner.

To their right, they saw the food stands offered homemade jerky, corn dogs, hamburgers, and corn on the cob. Next to the snowball stand, they saw the best pie and cake contest, to which Nell had submitted one of her pies—huckleberry.

The left side of the fair held contests dealing with livestock: horses, cows, goats, and sheep. Behind the pony and horse rides, Shannon found Ryan.

Ryan spoke to all of them once he'd spotted them, but he kept his eyes on Shannon. "Hey, I haven't seen you around. What have you ladies been doing? I was hoping you would come over to take a ride."

Shannon could feel the blush on her cheeks as she looked up at Ryan. "We went on some hikes and shopped and relaxed. Drove to the diner once or twice to eat, so we didn't have to cook. Took a ride down to the Indian reservation. I got some pottery and turquoise jewelry"

"Dad, I'm back." That came from a voice behind Ryan.

"Okay. Colby, this is Shannon and her friends. They're on vacation from Florida." Colby gave his father a look, but she sure didn't know what it meant. When she glanced up at Ryan, he had a scowl on his face for his son.

"Hello. Nice to meet you," he said before he turned and strolled away.

"Want to take a ride? I promise she'll be a smooth ride," Ryan promised.

There was no way Shannon would pass up that opportunity. "Absolutely."

Shannon followed Ryan over to a chestnut-colored Quarter Horse named Sundancer. Ryan proclaimed her to be a calm horse, and said they would love riding her. "She's not one of the horses that you're loaning out for rides?" she asked Ryan as they headed up to stroke Sundancer's mane.

"No. This is my daughter, Carly's, horse. She just got done showing her. Came in second." You could hear the pride in his voice.

"Who came in first? I missed seeing the horse contest." It was the one event she'd looked forward to, but they'd wanted to support Nell at the pie contest. Shannon and her friends had become very fond of Nell and loved her homemade huckleberry pie.

Ryan chuckled. "That would be my son, Colby. My boys are always competing with one another. If you look over there, you'll see Midnight." Midnight was a black Quarter Horse with a small white star on his forehead. His coat shined like black silk. By the time he explained, he already had Sundancer saddled and ready to go. He even had a lead rope ready.

"Ryan, I don't need a lead rope. I know how to ride." She didn't try to hide her annoyance at him holding the lead rope. Lead ropes were typically used with those who didn't know how to ride.

Ryan turned to Shannon with a surprised look on his face. "I know you can ride, but it's part of the rules with the fairgrounds. We have to lead the horses around the enclosure so no one gets hurt… for insurance purposes."

"Oh, I'm sorry." She flushed with embarrassment because of her snappy remark. Without saying anything else, she mounted the horse and attached the reins to the saddle horn. Shannon leaned forward and patted the horse on the side of her neck.

Ryan guided the horse around the

enclosure twice. After she dismounted, he gave a ride to Lisa and Erica. It took some convincing to get Bianca on the horse, but the girls finally got their friend on Sundancer. Ryan went around slower with Bianca than the rest of their group, because she was so skittish about being on a horse. When he got back, Shannon took one more ride. Ryan was only too happy to give her a ride. She would love to ride more than his horse.

When he got back with Shannon her friends and Steve stood together, talking. Before Shannon dismounted, Ryan placed his hand on her knee. "I would love to have you and your friends come out to the ranch. We can go for a ride, bring lunch out to the lake I have on my property, and go swimming, too. What do you say?"

Shannon was about to answer when she heard, "Dad, Sundancer isn't part of the horse rides. I brought her here to show her, not to ride her. I don't like strange people on *my* horse."

Ryan slowly turned around to face his daughter, the muscle jumping in his jaw. Shannon could tell that he didn't appreciate her tone or manner. From the look on his daughter's face, she knew that she'd gone too far.

"Sundancer may be your horse…that I paid for, but it's *my* ranch, and my money that takes care of her, and you haven't ridden her in months. Don't you ever talk to me like that again. Are we clear?" Ryan looked really annoyed and his expression showed he wouldn't back down.

Carly cut a glance to Shannon then her father. "Yes, sir. I'm sorry." She rushed off, heading to join Colby who stood a short distance away and clearly saw the whole thing.

After taking a deep breath, Ryan helped Shannon down.

Ryan told Shannon about what kind of horses he had and set off over to her friends. Steve decided that he would join them tomorrow. Shannon noticed that Steve stood close to Erica. The guys asked what they'd seen so far and what they'd enjoyed the most. They decided that they would all get something to eat. Shannon felt Ryan place his hand on her lower back as they went to order food.

* * *

Carly and Colby watched their father leave and when he placed his hand on Shannon's back, Carly reached out and gripped Colby's arm. "Did you see that? Why is he touching her? He's married. Who is she? I need to call Mom." She began to take out her phone.

Colby reached over and took her phone away before she did something she would regret. When she started to yell at him, he interrupted her. "Carly, for one, Mom and Dad aren't married anymore. If he wants to date or flirt it's his business, not yours. You need to stop trying to get them back together. It's not going to happen. I just met her a little while ago. Her name is Shannon, and they're here on vacation. Steve is renting one of his cabins to them."

"But, Mom and Dad loved each other once. They can do it again."

"No. It's been over for three years. Stay out of it, sis. Don't you call Mom. Besides, she's in L.A. with what's his name," Colby reminded her as he placed his arm around his sister and squeezed. "I need to get back to help Dustin give everyone rides. Leave it, sis." He kissed the top of her head and headed back to where his brother waited for him.

She watched her brother lope away. *I'm calling Mom. There has to be way to get Mom to come here.* Carly planned to get her parents together if it was the last thing she did. Her father wasn't going to be with anyone but her mother.

Her mom's cell phone went right to voicemail. "Mom, you need to call me or come here right away. It's Dad. Some woman is after him, and I know all she'll do is hurt him. Please call me back. I need your help." *Well, that should do it. Now I just have to wait for her to call me back.*

* * *

"Are you going to stay for the music and dancing?" Ryan asked Shannon.

Lisa looked at Ryan and Steve. "We're planning to. Are you guys going to be around?"

After agreeing to stay together and listen to listen to music, they wandered around to find a place to sit down. Shannon watched as Ryan's children passed them about four times, but didn't stop by to talk to them.

"Do you only have the two children? I heard you had two boys." Shannon wanted to know more about Ryan. She shouldn't. Her heart couldn't take being broken again.

Ryan explained, "I have twin boys, but they're fraternal twins. You met my daughter. I'm sorry for what happened." He leaned back on his elbow. "My sons help with the ranch and will take over one day, I hope. Not sure what Carly is going to do. Maybe go to college."

Shannon turned to see Ryan. "My son, Dylan... I worry about him most of all. The military is a career for him, but what happens if he gets deployed? I know he's well-trained, but that doesn't matter to me. I'm his mom, and I still worry. In a way, I hope he doesn't re-enlist. You must think that's selfish of me to say." Fear twisted her gut at the thought of something happening to her son if he got deployed.

"No. If it was one of my sons or even my daughter, I wouldn't want them deployed. I enjoy having them close to me. I don't know how the hell you do it," Ryan stated.

"I try not to think about it and I don't watch the news." Shannon couldn't believe that she was opening up to Ryan. It felt right and made her feel lighter, too. Ryan didn't make her feel that she had no right to worry or make the remarks that some made. Like, 'He's well-trained so don't worry' or 'You shouldn't be surprised. He's in the military.'

The music played into the night and people danced everywhere. Frank, Nell, Max, Mitch, and JP joined them as the evening wore on. JP sat next to Lisa, and Max and Mitch perched on either side of Bianca. Ryan leaned into Shannon to whisper into her ear. "Want to take a walk?"

She nodded and Ryan helped Shannon to stand. "Hey, we'll be back," she told her friends.

They walked in silence through the fairgrounds, but it wasn't uncomfortable. The quiet relaxed her after all the stimulation of the day. When they reached the other side of the park, Ryan led her to a bench surrounded by pine trees.

They sat side by side, enjoying the night, the sounds from the fair, and the wildlife. The slight chill to the air made Shannon glad she'd worn jeans and a flannel shirt over her V-neck t-shirt. She didn't know what to say since they were alone. Ryan broke the ice. "So, did you have fun today?"

"Yes. Your community really gets involved. It's nice to see how other places do things." She felt like a high schooler on a first date instead of a grown woman, widowed, with two adult children. She glanced at him from the corner of her eye and wondered what his lips would feel like against her skin. Would he taste as good as he looked? *What is wrong with this damn picture?* A shiver ran through her at her thoughts.

Ryan must have thought she was cold, because he moved closer and placed his arm around her. "I guess I should've brought a blanket for you."

No way she would admit why she shivered after that, because she liked having his strong muscular arm around her. Shannon inhaled his scent—horse, hay, and spice. The combination stirred a desire inside her that she hadn't felt in years.

"I'm good. Thank you," was all she could think to say.

Ryan turned slightly to look at her. "When you all come over tomorrow, I can take the wagon for Bianca since she's skittish around horses."

"You have a wagon? Really?" Shannon couldn't believe that ranches still used wagons.

Ryan's smile warmed her as much as the husky timbre of his voice. "Yeah, of course. Sometimes we have to move the cattle or horses to the other side of the property. So, we take out the equipment in the wagon and camp out. If the fence needs repairs, we load up the wagon with everything we might need."

She nodded. It made sense. "We're going to go to the next town with Nell and have a girls' day out. Frank gave Nell the day off to go with us. Or Nell just told him she's going." She smiled at the idea of Nell telling someone five-ten to her five-one that she's going out and taking the day off.

"Well, how about the next day? Do you have anything going on?" The hope in his voice came through loud and clear.

Thankfully, she agreed. "That sounds great. Lunch it is. I'll call you sometime tomorrow to get directions. I guess we need to head back."

Ryan stood and offered his hand to help her up. Once she was on her feet, he said, "First, I need to do this."

He leaned in then brushed his lips across Shannon's once, twice, then licked her bottom lip. When she opened slightly, he surged forward and entered her mouth with his tongue. She tasted the huckleberry from the pie they ate earlier. He pulled back first, and looked deeply into her eyes. "You taste wonderful. I could kiss you all day." He started to rest his forehead against hers.

"I haven't been kissed like that in years," she admitted.

Ryan smiled, showing dimples that she hadn't noticed until then. "Then maybe I should kiss you again." He straightened and moved his hands down her arms until he could intertwine their fingers. She leaned into him, smelling his scent again, spicy and a hint of...ocean breeze. "If we don't move soon, I'm not sure if I will let you go."

Shannon pulled back and let go of one of Ryan's hands. Going back, hand and hand, through the fair, she noticed most of the booths had closed and people were leaving. She noticed Ryan's children watching as they joined her friends. Sneaking a glance at Ryan, she noticed he saw his children and the look on his face made them turn the other direction.

"Hey, man, there you are. Where have you been?" Steve asked Ryan. The man's face creased with a small smile when he noticed them holding hands.

Ryan pushed Steve in the shoulder and whispered, "Not a word." Shannon ducked her head, turning to her friends.

They cleaned up the area where they'd sat and started toward their cars to head back to the cabin. Shannon wished the distance to their car would take longer, but they'd parked close to the fair. "So, I will see you the day after tomorrow. I'll call you to get the time to show up."

Should she kiss him or just say good night?

He made the decision for her when he turned her toward him to kiss her tenderly on her lips. It was just a slight brush against her lips. She felt a crack in the shield she'd built around her heart to protect it.

With a small curve of his lips, she said, "Talk to you tomorrow."

He followed Steve to his truck and, damn, did he look good in those jeans from the back. She couldn't help but admire his wide shoulders, trim waist, and fantastic ass.

"Earth to Shannon. Come in, Shannon. You can stare at his ass later. Let's go!" Erica must be tired or pissed off, as she only got like that when she wanted to go to bed or punch someone.

Shannon rode in silence. She was lost in thoughts about Ryan and wanting to go see him and his ranch tomorrow instead of going shopping. When they got to the cabin, Shannon said, "I'm really tired and need to shower and go to bed." She really wanted to be alone and think. Shannon dropped into bed and fell right to sleep.

She sat on the bench in the woods in only her bra and panties. Ryan came up to her, totally naked. Oh my, and did he look yummy. She wanted to taste his skin. He pulled her to her feet, cupping the back of her head, and buried his fingers in her hair. His head bent down, and he brushed his firm, full, sexy lips back and forth over hers. With a gasp, he urged her to open for him and Shannon gladly complied. He dove deeper into her mouth, devouring her taste. No one had ever kissed her and fired up her blood like Ryan. All she wanted to do was rub herself all over him.

His tongue danced with hers as he rubbed her nipple with his thumb and forefinger over her bra. His other hand left her hair and slowly moved inside her panties until he slid a finger into her. He heated up parts of her that she thought died with her husband.

Shannon pulled back, wanting to rub her hands up his biceps to his shoulders then move them to his chest and over his nipples that hardened at her touch. Ryan had six-pack abs that made her mouth water. Her fingers ran along his ribs. Her thumbs moved down the middle until reaching his navel. His breathing grew faster as her hands went lower.

Her hands moved over his hips, but instead of moving lower, she pulled back and moved around to his back, running a hand over his tight ass. Gliding up to his lower back and up to his shoulder blades and wide shoulders. Shannon then placed open-mouthed kisses and licked her way in a trail down the center of his back.

Lowering to her knees, she gripped his muscled thighs and gently turned him around. She continued to slide her hands from the back of his knees up his thighs until she reached his hard cock.

Shannon jerked awake, bathed in sweat, hot and very horny. *Shit, shit, shit.* It was the second time she'd woke up in one night from dreaming about Ryan naked and hard.

Well, she wasn't going to try to go back to bed. Off to take another shower… a very cold shower.

FIVE

Not being able to see Shannon drove Ryan crazy. He called Shannon's cell and left a message for her to call him back when she had a chance. Then he sent her a text with his address, home phone number, and cell number again.

He'd been late to breakfast that morning because Shannon haunted his dreams. He'd woke up three times in a hot sweat and so hard it was painful. Cold showers didn't help one damn bit.

Once he finally made it to the stables, he wasn't in any mood for the looks his sons gave him. They obviously had a problem with him or seeing him with Shannon. Probably the latter.

"Who was the lady with you at the fair?" Dustin asked with a pissed off attitude as he peeked into the stall. Ryan didn't care for the tone in his voice.

Turning to meet his son's eyes, he said, "Let me see… I don't think I owe you an answer to that. Especially if you think you can take that tone with me. So, you best watch that damn mouth of yours."

Colby came into the stall with them. "What's going on?" He looked back and forth between his father and brother. Colby was always the one trying to calm tempers. He's like Ryan; however, when Ryan got mad all hell broke loose.

Silence filled the air around them. Their mother was on boyfriend number three… or four? He'd lost count. Why him being interested in a woman was a problem was beyond him. They couldn't think that, after so much time passed, that he would get back together with Vicky. That part of his life was over. Hell, they'd been over before they even started, but the kids didn't need to know that. Still, Ryan didn't regret the time they had shared, if only because of his children.

"Look, son, do I get involved when you date? No. In fact, I have no idea who or if you are dating." Ryan felt like he was trying hard to reason with them, perhaps even more than he should have to, really. "But her name is

Shannon, and she's here on vacation from Florida. We haven't gone out on an official date yet, even. For right now, that is all you need to know, unless you plan on telling me about your sex lives."

Ryan notice Dustin looking at Colby for help. He knew Colby would stay out of it. "That's okay." He turned to go to the next stall that needed cleaning.

"Before you all come in for dinner tonight, get the small wagon out for tomorrow. We have clients coming for lunch by the lake and horseback riding. Steve, JP, and I will be taking them out. Max and Mitch might be coming, too." Ryan didn't know why those two wanted to come, but he really didn't care.

Dustin turned to his father and looked calmer. "Colby and I normally take the clients out. You all don't have to go out. That's what you have us here for."

Shit, he would have to let them know why. "Shannon and her friends are the clients. So yes, I'm taking them out."

"Who are you taking out?" That came from his daughter, Carly. "Is it that woman from the fair yesterday? You can't be serious. What is Mom going to say? You with some other woman?" Carly started raising her voice.

Why, oh, why are my kids acting like this?

Ryan turned very slowly to face his daughter. He took note that Colby whispered something in her ear, and that she'd just realized what she'd just done. "One, who I see is none of your damn business. Your mom and I will *never* get back together or get remarried. You need to understand this, Carly, and you *will* watch your attitude with me. Vicky has no say in who I date, just like I don't get involved with who she is seeing," Ryan admonished his daughter.

"Yes, sir." She turned and left without another word.

"You two. Let's get done." The strength in Ryan's voice let them know that there would be no more questions. He looked at the now empty space where his daughter had stood. *I need to talk to her alone. I don't like being at odds with my kids.*

The three of them worked through the stalls and the rest of the chores without any more comments about Shannon and her friends. He headed up to the house for lunch along with his boys. As they got closer to the house he saw his daughter on the phone, getting into her car to head to work. *Shit, she's already leaving for work. Okay, I'll send her a text and let her know we need to talk.*

* * *

Carly got into her car to go to work. She tried to call her mother again, but she didn't pick up the phone and it went to voicemail.

"Mom, you have got to call me back. Some woman is trying to get close to Dad, and I don't trust her. Please call me back or come out to the ranch." She hung up phone and left for work. She had to get her mother to come to see dad. She knew that she could get them back together. *It just has to work.*

* * *

Shannon and her friends, along with Nell, went to the mall in the next town. Nell took them to this western store that she loved. They all found items that they couldn't live without, each gorgeous with a western flair.

They ate lunch at the eatery in the mall. Joking around with Nell, Lisa leaned back into her chair. "I don't know, Nell. Are you sure Frank will wear a red shirt?"

Chuckling at the surprise on Nell's face. Shannon had to add, "Maybe he'll claim it's too small. And you'll have to help him out of it." That was all it took for Erica to start singing, "No Shoes, No Shirt, No Problem," by Kenny Chesney.

They all picked up a French fry and tossed

them at Erica, who was now laughing hysterically. Which got all of them laughing right with her.

Nell was finally able to say, "Even if he doesn't like it, he'll wear it anyway because I got it for him. Of course, it doesn't hurt that he loves me, too."

"I'm thinking about staying at the cabin tomorrow instead of going horseback riding," Bianca mumbled to Shannon out of the blue.

Shannon looked at her in shock. "Oh, you will not. Ryan told me that he has a wagon and is planning on taking it. You can ride in the wagon." She had received two message and three texts from Ryan about tomorrow. He'd mentioned that they would be taking the wagon for Bianca and the coolers, so she wouldn't have to get on a horse.

Bianca looked down, clearly embarrassed. "He's not taking the wagon because of me, is he? I don't want to be a burden."

"Of course not. He'll have the coolers, blankets, chairs, and whatever else he needs. He's taking lunch for all of us. We can even go swimming in the lake." It pissed Shannon off to no end that Bianca was so unsure about herself. *That ex-boyfriend of hers, Mia's father, the asshole, always made her feel bad, worthless, and ugly.*

Heading to the children's store after lunch to look for a souvenir for Mia from their trip, Shannon noticed several men looking at Bianca and she thought about saying something. But she would never believe Shannon if she tried. She had a feeling that the bouncers from *After Hours* were interested in Bianca, too. Wondering if they would be coming tomorrow, she sent a text to Ryan to find out. She only sent the text to find out who was going, not because she wanted to hear from him. *Keep telling yourself that. You might start to believe it.*

After finding something for Mia, they decided they would head back to the cabin. On the way home they talked about going to the ranch, and Nell told them a little about daily life there. "Ryan and his boys are really good with the horses. His great-grandparents started the ranch, but Ryan has done more for the land and animals than anyone. There are two barns, two storage sheds, a bunkhouse, and two ranch houses. His boys live in the original house, and Ryan lives in the house he built when he took over the ranch."

Shannon wanted to ask more questions about the ranch, but didn't want them to know that she was interested. But Lisa knew her too well, and kept Nell talking about Ryan, his friends, and anything else she could think of asking. She listened intently to everything that Nell said, wanting to know about Ryan, but from a different point of view. Lisa asked if any of them were dating anyone. She was delighted that the answer to that question was "No."

Her phone chimed, letting her know that she'd received a text. When she pulled it out, she noticed she had two unread texts — one from her daughter and another from Ryan. She read her daughter's text first.

Wanted to check in. Hope all is well and you're having fun. Give me a call if you have time. Tell everyone hello for me. Love ya.

Shannon sent a quick text back. She knew she needed to respond to her fast, or else she would start calling.

Having a great time. Out shopping. Going horseback riding tomorrow. Text you again soon. Love you.

Next, the text from Ryan.

Yes, they're coming. They'll be guiding the wagon. Mitch doesn't want Bianca to know, because he's worried she may not show up. Can't wait to see you and everyone else.

He was right about one thing — Bianca would make sure she wasn't there if she knew that Mitch and Matt would be going. *Well, I'm not going to be the one to tell her.* She sent a quick text back.

I won't tell her. Looking forward seeing the ranch. And you, too.

Before she knew it, they pulled up to *After Hours*. "I didn't know we were stopping here."

Nell looked confused. "Frank is going to pick me up here, so I thought we could have a drink together while I wait. Is that okay?"

"That would be wonderful," Shannon answered as they all got out of the car.

Matt spotted them first when they got inside. "Hello, Bianca. I didn't know you ladies would be coming tonight."

Bianca blushed as she passed him to follow everyone to the table. Terry, a waitress, wrote down everyone's drink order while JP talked to everyone. They told him about their day then he looked at Nell. "Do you need me to take you home or is Frank coming? Bianca, are you going to be driving, since you didn't order a drink?"

Nell rolled her eyes at her cousin. "Of course he's coming to pick me up. You worry too much."

"Yes, I'll be driving," Bianca answered him at the same time Nell did.

"Okay. I'm just checking. I'll see you all tomorrow then." JP looked at Lisa with a wink.

Frank arrived shortly after their drinks arrived. They listened to Frank tell stories about some of the customers who came into the diner. And the college kids that showed up from the town west of them going to campgrounds to party.

"I swear I don't remember eating that much food in high school. Each one of the guys ate two bacon cheeseburgers with a double order of fries. And don't forget the pie. Sorry, there's no pie or cake left. Jodi, the poor girl, had the table. The only good thing was that they left her one hell of a tip." Frank leaned in, kissing Nell's temple. "Very busy and tiring day. Missed having you there, baby."

Nell blushed while Frank smiled devilishly and winked. Shannon couldn't be happier for Nell; to be loved that much warms your heart and lifts your soul.

When they were all done with their drinks, Nell said, "Thank you for inviting me to go with you. I had so much fun. We'll need to do this again."

Lisa piped up, "You got it, girlfriend." Shannon just chuckled along with everyone else.

"God help us all, with the five of you together," Frank added

Erica started to sing "Good Time" by Alan Jackson. Everyone picked up a pretzel and tossed it at her.

Waving goodbye, they all got into their cars and headed back to the cabin. Everyone was quiet on the ride. Walking into the cabin, Shannon said, "I'm tired. Going to shower and head to bed. See you all in the morning."

"I'm going straight to bed. I'll shower in the morning." Bianca headed up the stairs first.

Erica said, "Lisa and I are going to watch some television and then head up."

"Okay. See ya. Goodnight." Shannon headed to the shower. After the shower, she opened to door to the room that Bianca shared with her.

"So, what are you wearing tomorrow?" Bianca asked.

Shannon twisted around. "Jeans and a t-shirt. I'm going to wear my bathing suit underneath. You?"

"The same I think. Or I may wear my sundress over my bathing suit, since I'll be riding in the wagon." Bianca rolled to her side to look at Shannon. "What are you going to do about Ryan? I know you like him."

Sitting on the bed across from her, Shannon confessed, "I don't know. I shouldn't want to be with him. I can't just betray Tom."

Bianca sat up and crossed her legs on the bed. "Do you think that he would want you to be alone for the rest of your life? Would you want him to be if, God forbid, something had happened to you? You deserve to be happy. Let someone else in, Shannon. You can love more than one man. Just think about it."

"I will. Goodnight, Bianca. Pleasant dreams." Shannon lay down, thinking about everything Bianca said. *What am I going to do?*

SIX

The next morning, Ryan ate breakfast with his sons. "Everything ready with the horses and wagon?"

"Yes. Everything is out. The horses haven't been stabled yet. We can wait until they get here to pull them out in the sun." Ryan's heart surged with pride. Colby was always on top of things.

The front door opened and the rest of his buddies entered the kitchen. "I have arrived. Let the party begin!" Steve had a huge smile on his face.

"The girls should be here soon. Cool your heels," Ryan answered.

Everyone started laughing at Steve when he placed his hand over his heart and acted pained.

Ryan had told Shannon about the horse, but didn't know if he'd explained that his cattle were Black Angus. He had some Quarter Horses, Appaloosas, Paint horses and one horse that was half Tennessee Walker, half Quarter Horse. In the corral, Ryan's black and white Appaloosa stood guard, his head raised and his ear cocked forward as he watched over the land, protecting what he believed was his.

When the group pulled up to the house, they waited for them on the front porch. Ryan saw Bianca's eyes widen at the sight of Mitch and Matt.

Once he reached Shannon's side, he asked, "Would you like to see the barn with the horses? I know you must be looking forward to it. I can see it written all over your face." He chuckled.

"Yes, please. I feel like a kid getting my first look at a horse." She fell into step, following him toward the barn. "This is your idea of a barn? It's huge." Pride surged at her stunned expression and beaming smile.

"Yes, the barn is double the size of most. I have seven stalls on one side and six stalls on the other. The other space on that side is an open storage area that holds the ropes, blankets, reins, and saddles for the horses.

Across from that is a grooming area with the brushes, combs, sweat scraper, and picks to clean the hooves. The stalls across from the storage are filled with hay on one side and barrels that hold the oat feed." Ryan showed off his space with pride.

"Most of the horses are in the corral. But I do have some of them in their stalls." He knew she would wonder where all the horses were. Shannon walked over to a stall that had a nameplate that read 'Trigger', the home of a buckskin-colored Quarter Horse. Next to him was Midnight's stall, a black Quarter Horse. "Trigger is Dustin's horse. He only lets Colby on him, because he has a bad attitude. Midnight is Colby's. Almost anyone can ride him, if he's in a good mood."

"They're beautiful. When we drove up I saw an Appaloosa. What's his name?" Shannon asked, without looking at Ryan because at that moment Midnight trotted over and hung his head over the stall door.

"That beast would be Thunder. He's mine and won't let anyone ride him but me. His name suits him because the damn horse loves storms. Stupid, but he does, and he watches over everything going on. Let's go out to the fence and I'll call him for you."

Standing by the fence, Ryan reached inside

his pocket and pulled out a quarter of an apple. "Here, take this." After he handed it to her, he whistled loudly.

They couldn't see, but they could hear Thunder running to the barn. He was a gorgeous horse. When he spotted Ryan, the animal slowed down to a trot and stopped when he got close. "Go on and show the beast what you got. Look, Thunder."

He watched as Shannon held her hand out flat so her fingers wouldn't be mistaken for a carrot or anything edible. "Here you go, boy. Look what I've got for you," Shannon encouraged.

Thunder leaned in, smelling her hand, then took a step forward and took the piece of apple out of her hand. After he ate it he nodded his head up and down, snorting air out of his nose, and stomped his right leg in the dirt. Shannon laughed when he then started to rub his head against her shirt, obviously looking for more food.

Ryan couldn't hide his surprise. "Well, this is a first. He must like you. Thunder has never done this to anyone before."

"Hey, man, you ready to head out?" JP asked as he joined them. "You haven't saddled Thunder yet. Come on, by the time we get to the lake it will be past noon."

JP, Steve, Max, and Ryan worked together to finish getting the rest of the horses saddled. Rosa, his housekeeper, had Mitch hauling the coolers that she'd filled. Of course, she had to come out and see who was there. Rosa had overheard Steve and him talking about the ride and Shannon the night before. So, she knew that Ryan planned on asking Shannon out on a date today.

Rosa came up to Ryan, "Is there anything else you need?"

Ryan leaned in and chuckled in her ear. "You trying to find out which one she is, aren't you?" When he stood up straight, she lightly slapped his arm while he laughed.

Hank, her husband and Ryan's foreman, came over. "Are you putting your nose where it doesn't belong?" He smiled down at his wife and placed an arm around her.

"Oh, you stop it. I want to know what one has Ryan's attention," Rosa said, trying to be serious.

Ryan called everyone over and made the introductions. He made sure to save Shannon for last, just to torture Rosa. Rosa shook her hand and gave Shannon a big smile. She turned and patted Ryan's arm, still smiling as she went back to the house. *Well, she likes Shannon at least.*

Ryan, Shannon, Erica, and Steve hopped into their saddles. The wagon followed next, with Mitch guiding the horse along with Max and Bianca. That left JP and Lisa to bring up the rear.

As they rode out to the lake, Ryan could tell Shannon admired the scenery. Every so often, someone made a comment or asked a question. The mountains, which looked small from the ranch, grew the closer to them. They still had some snow on their peaks. He would love to climb up there with her and throw snowballs just to see what she would do. The scent of the horses, wildflowers, and forest hung in the air around them. A slight breeze whispered down from the mountain and tried telling them a secret that they couldn't quite hear.

Ryan pointed in the distance. Pronghorns grazed in the field, making sure they stayed close to the forest line for easy escape. Black-Billed Magpies flew by, looking for food. He appreciated the peace surrounding them. Listening to the wildlife around him, the horses making noises, and the whispering of the wind soothed his soul. Birds called back, answering the whispers. He would love for Shannon to be a part of his world every day.

Ryan could read the expression on her face. "Breathtaking, isn't it? You should see it out here at night. Fireflies light up the area. The moonlight shines off the lake that I'm taking you to. Even though I don't want the wolves to kill my animals, I do love to hear them howling to one another. I imagine that they're telling each other it's safe to come out and play. The bears and sometimes the cubs get ready to sleep or find food. This is Mother Nature at her best."

Shannon didn't say anything, just looked at him and smiled the most beautiful smile he had ever seen. Her whole face lit up and her eyes sparkled like diamonds. He would do anything to make sure that expression never left her face. *Fuck. What the hell.*

"Okay. I'm going act like a teenager, here. Are we there yet?" Erica yelled to make sure everyone heard her. She started singing that phrase over and over.

Everyone laughed at her. Most of them yelled back, "No." Ryan was the one who ended up giving a more specific answer. "The lake is over the next rise."

Steve came up behind Ryan's horse. "Don't you fuckin' do it, Steve." Before he could finish his sentence, Steve gave Thunder a smack on his ass and he took off. Steve raced after him, followed by JP, hooting and hollering.

"What are they? Ten?" Lisa asked. Ryan heard Lisa's question and at the same time the sound of two additional horses running his way: Shannon and Erica. Now, this was the most fun Ryan had in a very long time.

Stopping at the top of the rise, they looked down at the lake. "Well, Erica, you're here." Ryan gave Shannon a wink and finished galloping down to the lake.

They all joined Ryan and he told them to tie up the horses. Steve and JP took off the saddles and blankets to give the horses a rest. Ryan fed them and made sure the square wooden bucket had fresh water. Mitch and Max got the coolers, blankets, and towels out of the wagon. Ryan went into a small storage shed that sat between two pine trees and brought out chairs.

The lake was so clear Ryan knew that they would be able to see the bottom. There was a small wooden dock with an area for chairs. On the left by the shed, one of the trees had a rope tied to it and almost to the bottom was a knot with a space for feet. "I haven't seen a rope swing since I lived in Maryland."

"The picnic table isn't here. The boys have to replace some of the wood," Ryan explained.

Shannon helped set up the chairs. "This is really nice. You guys come out here a lot?"

"We used to come out more, but we all try to get together at least twice a month now. Someone, who I will not mention, has been an ass about not getting together," Steve stated firmly.

Ryan turned his head. "Shut the fuck up, asshole." He had no heat behind the comment and it was said low enough for Steve's ears only, as more of a joke.

Bianca passed Ryan. "Mia would love this." She obviously missed her daughter. "I don't think I could get her to go into the water. The dock, yes." He watched her follow Lisa to the dock.

"Why won't she go in? Can't she swim?" Matt asked. He looked concerned that Bianca's little girl wouldn't go swimming.

Shannon answered, "It's a long story. To shorten it, Mia had an accident in a pool and lost part of her hearing. She hasn't gone into the water since. Bianca doesn't force the issue, either. Can I help out with anything?"

Ryan picked up on the tension and Shannon redirecting the conversation, so he tried to lighten the mood. "Why don't we all sit down and eat? I'm starving." Placing his hand on Shannon's lower back, he guided her to the blanket and chairs that they had set up. He gave his friend the 'shut up' look.

They all sat down to eat the sandwiches, potato salad, and fruit salad that Rosa packed for them.

Ryan wanted to learn as much as he could about them... well, about Shannon.

"I work in the accounting department at a bank. Bianca works in bakery. Lisa is an administrative assistant for an advertising firm, and Erica works as a secretary for a real estate company," Shannon informed them.

"We get together and go to the movies or the beach or shopping, when we get together," Lisa added.

"Don't forget the trips to Disney for Mia. Oh, the zoo, the parks, and miniature golfing." That came from Bianca.

Lisa added, "We also go to all the craft fairs and other events."

The girls were close, but they always did something so Bianca's daughter, Mia, would be able to attend.

Over the course of the conversation, Ryan realized that Shannon didn't watch a lot of TV and loved to be outside. "I do go horseback riding in the wintertime. We've even went canoeing on Peace River once."

As if you could call winter in Florida cold. Ryan kept that thought to himself.

Mia, Bianca's daughter, was clearly loved by everyone. He could tell by the way their faces lit up when talking about the little girl.

"Does she see her father?" Mitch asked Bianca.

Shannon answered, "No. He's isn't involved, and that's for the best."

He noticed Mitch and Max looking at each other and then at Bianca with interest. He swore that the twins could hold a whole conversation with one look; just like his boys.

The guys had their swimsuits on under their jeans. They all decided to get ready to go into the lake. They set up the towels on a tree branch to give the girls some privacy.

Ryan knew they would all see the scars on his back when his shirt came off. When they all got back to the towels, Ryan looked at everyone, "I remember the time my parents let me go riding without them. I had a Quarter Horse named Bullet. Anyway, I took off when I knew the weather was declining. The storm came and Bullet took off with me on him. He ended up throwing me right into the barbed wire fence. Took my parents hours to find me. Rushed me to the hospital with deep gashes on my back. That move left me with permanent scars." Then he took off his shirt and turned around.

It was JP who spoke first. "I remember that. You wouldn't take off your shirt in front of us for years."

"How long did it take for you to get on a horse again?" Ryan wasn't too surprised the question came from Bianca.

"To be honest? Two weeks. But, my parents didn't let me go out without them for a couple of months. I couldn't give up on something I love to do. It wasn't that easy the first day, but I made myself do it," Ryan answered after turn back to them.

He heard Shannon. "I'm sorry that happened to you, but glad you didn't stop doing what you obviously love to do and are good at."

"You should've seen Ryan when he jumped in the lake once and his swimsuit came off. We were in middle school and had some girls here, too. That was hilarious. He almost blinded us with that white ass of his," Steve told them, wanting to change the mood.

"That's enough, Steve." But Ryan's interruption didn't stop him. Steve and JP stood up, taunting him. Ryan got up, along with Matt, and the four of them started to wrestle until they all ended up in the lake.

Eventually everyone ended up in the lake,

splashing each other. The guys got out, grabbed the rope swing, and did cannon balls into the lake. The five of them tried to outdo one another and that made them laugh even harder. They all acted like a bunch of teenagers. Shannon and her friends rated each trick the guys did, and the guys would argue if they didn't like the scores or comments.

The girls wanted to show them how it was done. They not only did cannon balls, but turned and twisted in the air before hitting the water. The girls received higher scores than the guys. They swam around and splashed each other.

Something caught Ryan's eye and he headed for the dock. Bianca was sitting on a towel, watching everyone else having fun. Kneeling down, he said, "You got out of the water early. You okay?"

Shrugging her shoulder, she answered, "Yes, I'm good. It's absolutely beautiful here. I love the mountains... the peacefulness and clean air."

Sitting down next to her, he bent one knee and rested on his hand. "Thanks. It is."

Glancing over at Ryan, she said, "She's trying to fight the attraction she feels for you. She worries that being with you is betraying Tom and what they had. They loved each other dearly, and when he died a piece of her died, too. But, normally time should heal that hole. Instead of letting it heal, she built walls around her heart. You're going to have to rip them down. That won't be easy."

Not wanting to say much, in the hope that Bianca would give him some for insight, he said, "It's coming down. To stay."

"You're going to have to push, Ryan. She'll back off and close down fast if she thinks you're getting close. She has laughed and smiled more than I've seen in years. Make her happy again, love her, and get that wall down so she can love someone other than us and her children."

Both of them turned their heads when Ryan heard Lisa calling for Bianca. "I'm coming!" Bianca hollered back. Ryan went to help her up. "Ryan, just don't hurt her. I don't ever want to see her in that much pain again." Bianca's eyes filled with tears.

"Bianca, I have no intention of hurting her. That I can promise. I will get through. Thank you for trusting and believing in me... even though you don't know me that well."

Wiping away a tear, she said, "I can tell just by the way you stare at her that you're falling for my friend."

Mitch and Matt had concerned looks on their faces. Before reaching their friends, he said, "You know, you have a good heart and a pure soul. Just maybe you'll find love here, too."

Stopping, she faced Ryan. "That would take a miracle." Then she finished walking into the lake.

Ryan glanced at Mitch and Matt. "I think I can arrange the miracle you deserve."

Ryan dove into the water and swam over to Shannon. Going under the water, he stood up, putting Shannon on his shoulders. She laughed and held onto his hair. "Hang on."

Turning, he noticed Steve had Erica, JP had Lisa, and Mitch was getting Bianca onto his shoulders to play chicken. The girls laughed and screamed. Lisa was the first to fall off JP, but she took him under the water with her. Mitch at one point transferred Bianca to Matt's shoulders. Erica fell only because she covered Steve's eyes and Ryan tripped him.

It only left Shannon and Bianca, and the two of them wouldn't push each other off. Ryan mouthed to Matt, "Go under on three." With a nod from Matt he mouthed, "One, Two…" then Matt and Ryan went under the water, taking the girls with them.

Ryan came out of the water and got a face full of water. Shannon had a wide smile as they all walked out of the lake. "You two cheated. I didn't touch her."

"We knew you two wouldn't push the other, so we helped." Ryan picked up two other towels and handed her one.

Ryan noticed it was getting late and they all started to get cleaned up. Bianca nodded her head at him and mouthed, "Go."

He saw Shannon going over to the horses and decided it was his chance to talk to her alone. Coming up behind, her he gripped her waist. "I have a question."

"And what would that be?" She sounded a little breathless.

Gently, he turned her around. "Will you let me take you out to dinner?"

Ryan noticed her eyes widening as complete shock and confusion came over her face. He waited, wanting to give her time the think. Her lips parted and Ryan thought for sure by her scared look that a 'No' was next. Ryan noticed her taking a deep breath while her eyes sparkled and her face flushed. *She decided*. "Yes," was all that needed to be said.

SEVEN

The next day, she got a call from Ryan and found out he had to postpone their date for the following day. Apparently, Venus, a mix between Tennessee Walker and Quarter Horse, had gone into labor and was having a difficult time. She was having twins and he was a little worried, so he didn't want to leave her. She admired his loyalty to his horses.

Not wanting him to think that she was upset with him, she was quick to tell him, "I understand. I wouldn't want to leave her, either. I hope everything goes well. How about tomorrow?" What was she doing?

"Thank you for understanding. I'll pick you up for lunch. We can go to the diner. See you tomorrow, Shannon." He sounded tired. He must've been up for a long time.

"See you tomorrow, Ryan. I'll call you

later."

Later that day they all went to the bookstore, wanting to look around. Shannon wanted to sit outside and read a good book, but she didn't have a book with her, only magazines.

As they entered the bookstore, she noticed Ryan's daughter placing books on the shelf. "Hello, it's Carly, right?" Shannon said with a smile. "I'm looking for the romance novels?"

Carly just glared. Shannon wasn't sure if it was the question or her that Carly obviously didn't like. But by the closed off expression she had, Shannon knew she wouldn't be getting an answer.

Before Carly could answer, Mrs. Conway, the owner of the bookstore came out from the storage room. "Is there a problem here?"

Shannon spoke first. "No, I'm just wondering where the romance novels are kept. I can't seem to locate them."

"Oh, my. I need to fix the names on the shelves. I moved them to the front. Here, let me show you." Mrs. Conway showed Shannon and Bianca where the romance books were. Lisa and Erica were two rows over, looking at the mystery books.

Shannon glanced over the see Mrs. Conway

speaking softly to Carly. Boy, that girl didn't look happy at whatever the older lady said. She obviously had a problem with Shannon. Carly might not like the fact that she had a date with her father. Shannon didn't want to start a fight between Ryan and his kids. It was very important to her that, when and if she ever dated again, there would be no fight between the kids and parent.

Maybe she should cancel the date with Ryan, even though she didn't want to. She enjoyed his company and he was so easy to talk to. Even the silence between them was comfortable. They also had a lot in common. The most important ones were their love for their kids and horses.

Shannon loved riding her horse through the woods back home in Maryland. Being able to go places that a car couldn't go. Racing around the trees without having to hear the motor from a motorcycle or four wheelers. It was just freeing.

They all headed to the front to pay for the books that they'd picked out. Shannon paused when she handed her book to Carly. Carly said nothing and neither did she. She paid for the book and said goodbye, but Carly still didn't reply.

They walked down to the diner and

ordered coffee and four slices of pie to take back to the cabin. When they got the cabin, they relaxed on blankets outside, ate pie, talked for a while, then Shannon started to read her romance novel.

They all took turns cooking during the trip, and Shannon and Lisa would be cooking dinner that night. While they cooked she heard her cell phone go off, so she went to retrieve the phone. She saw a text from the Ryan.

Making sure we are still on for tomorrow. I'll pick you up at twelve o'clock to have lunch.

She quickly texted back. *I'll be ready.*

She hesitated to ask about the pregnant mare and the foals. It really wasn't any of her business, but she couldn't resist. *How is Venus doing?*

About half an hour later, he finally texted back. *Momma and babies are doing fine. Twin girls. Haven't named them yet. You'll see them tomorrow.*

That's great. See you tomorrow. Can't wait to see them. Shannon just stood there and stared at her phone, waiting for it to run off. She really was going to go out on a date with a man. *What am I doing? Do I really want to do this?*

Ryan was the typical tall, dark, and handsome. Well, he's fucking sexy in those tight jeans that hugged his ass. She loved his black Stetson, the way it shielded his eyes but didn't hide those lips that she loved to taste. He had blue-grey eyes that Shannon could drown in. Then she'd run her hands up over his blue flannel shirt that didn't hide his biceps because he stretched the seams apart. To top it off, he had those wide, strong shoulders, over the cords of his neck, to a strong jaw with the start of his five o'clock shadow. She would run her thumbs over his lower lip that she wanted to lick. More than anything, she wanted those lips on her; her neck, breasts…

She snapped herself out of that line of thinking and placed the phone in her back pocket just in case he sent a text later. She really tried to avoid looking at Lisa as she returned to the kitchen, but as she walked past Lisa tapped her shoulder.

"I'm sorry. Didn't mean to take so long. What?"

"You know what I want. So, spill."

Well, damn. "One of Ryan's horses had twins." She peeked at Lisa. *Shit, one hand on hip. She wants more info.* "We're going out on a date tomorrow. To the diner or lodge. For lunch."

"Keep on going, girlfriend." Lisa just stared at Shannon and waited.

"Nothing else to say." She turned around after she finished setting the table. "Okay, I haven't been on a date in forever. I'm getting a little nervous now. What am I going to do? What do I want with him? I like being around him and talking with him…" She looked up at one of her best friends for answers and advice.

Lisa faced Shannon. "Do you really think you can just ignore what you feel? You can't and you shouldn't. Go out with him. Have fun. Enjoy yourself." She walked over to Shannon and placed a hand on her shoulder. "He may be the one for you. But you won't know that unless you open your heart and just maybe find love again. Tom wouldn't want you to be alone forever."

She knew that Lisa was right, but she still felt like going on a date equaled cheating on her husband. Damn it, her *deceased* husband who she loved, had two wonderful children with, and raised them together. She wanted more in her life, and was still young enough to want to share it with someone. Maybe it would be Ryan, but she wouldn't know unless she dropped the walls around her heart and let someone in.

* * *

Rosa came into the kitchen and, to her surprise, found Ryan sitting at the table eating leftovers. "I thought you had a date tonight."

Ryan took a drink of his before answering. "I did, but with Venus having a hard time delivering the twins, I couldn't just leave her. Shannon and I rescheduled. We're going to the diner tomorrow for lunch. Then, I'm thinking about bringing her here to see Venus and the twin fillies."

"You didn't have to stay. Hank and your sons could have taken care of that horse, and you know it. You need to let your sons do more around here without you peering over their shoulders all the time." Rosa just stood there, glaring at him while she took him to task.

Chucking, he said, "Okay, okay. I got it. And, damn it, stop looking at me like that."

Rosa made her way to the back door to leave and head home to her husband. "You better clear up after yourself, Ryan Collins. And watch your mouth."

He had to holler before the door closed, "Yes, ma'am." Once she was gone, he laughed his ass off. Rosa had no problem telling anyone anything. Hank was one very lucky man.

He could only wish to have a wife like her. Vicky was a fucking pain in his ass from day one, especially after the boys were born. They should have ended it then, but he believed in his marriage vows and wanted to make it work. Plus, he had gotten her pregnant and then he did what was right. He had married her.

The hardest part of that time of his life was going to marriage counseling without letting anyone know. She didn't want the town or the boys to know about their problems. And, in one drunken night, after coming home from *After Hours,* he fucked said wife. He forgot to use a condom and got her pregnant again. He didn't regret it, because they made a beautiful baby girl. Carly.

They agreed to stay together until Carly hit high school. *What a long ass time.* They both slept in separate rooms. By the time Carly was in ninth grade, Vicky had pretty much moved out of the house. That's when they made it official and filed for divorce. Carly was the only one of the three kids that took the news hard. He had a feeling that she hoped they would get back together.

But Vicky hadn't told the kids yet is that she was engaged to be married. *Good luck to the man that she marries. He's going to need it.*

* * *

Ryan woke up early the next morning to check on the mare and the foals before he had to leave. He was happy to see everyone doing well. While he fed Thunder, his phone vibrated. He answered the call a little too rough, "Hello." *Damn.*

"Well, hello to you, too, asshole. Bad night with Shannon or didn't you get any?" Steve laughed his fool head off. *Dumbass.*

That just pissed him the fuck off. "That's none of your fucking business. And, no, I had to cancel my date with her last night because Venus went into labor and was having a rough time. We're going out today." And hopefully all night, too, but he wasn't going to tell his friend that.

"Damn, is she okay?" Ryan wasn't sure if he was talking about Shannon or the horse.

"Shannon was okay with changing the date. I told her I didn't want to leave without knowing if everything would be okay with the foals."

"Okay, well I'm glad Shannon was okay with the change, but I was talking about Venus, ass wipe." It was way too early for Steve to be up, and his sarcasm was starting to come out.

"Yes, all three are doing great. I just checked on them. What the hell is your problem? And why are you up so damn early?" Should Ryan be worried or not?

Steve took a deep breath before explaining, "Look, I wanted to let you know something. I went into town, checking on my business, and apparently Carly wasn't very friendly to the ladies. Especially Shannon. I'm not sure how your boys feel. You may want to talk to them, man, and soon."

Ryan wanted to strangle his kids. "Thanks, I will. Now, go back to bed because you need sleep so you aren't an asshole all day."

He ended the call and put both hands on Thunder's stall. "Damn it!" He was just starting to date again and his kids... He needed to talk to them and find out what was going on. *What the hell?*

"Is there a problem with Thunder?" *Well, let's start with my sons.*

When Ryan turned around, Dustin stood ramrod straight. "Thunder, Venus, and the foals are fine." As his son raised an eyebrow, Ryan continued. "Do you or your brother have a problem with Shannon? I want you to talk to me."

"Didn't know you were seeing her officially. So, what is going on?" Dustin shifted his feet, letting him know he was nervous. Ryan wasn't sure if his Dustin knew he shifted his feet when he was nervous or agitated about something.

Colby came around the corner just then and noticed his father and his brother. "Something going on that I need to know about?" Colby rubbed his thumb inside his hand, his nervous habit. But, unlike Dustin, Colby knew. When Ryan looked up at Colby he turned red and shoved his hands into his front pockets.

"I'll ask you the same thing I just asked Dustin. Do you have a problem with Shannon? If you do, talk to me. Please remember, however, that I don't answer to any of you."

Colby's eyes widened, "I only saw her briefly, Dad. I don't have a problem and neither does Dustin. Are you dating her?"

Colby was always the calm and reasonable one. "Yes, we're going on a date today, and she'll be here to see Venus. It would be nice of the two of you to stop by and say hello. But only if you can be nice."

"We will. Won't we, bro?" Colby elbowed Dustin. Dustin just nodded his head.

He didn't worry about Colby; he went with the flow. But Dustin was completely opposite. He didn't like change and it took time for him. Taking off his Stetson to run his fingers though his hair in frustration, he chuckled to himself; that was *his* nervous habit.

"I don't like the tension. We have always been able to talk when the three of you had issues, so I'm not understanding why we have a problem now. I'm here when you're ready to vent. But, remember one thing: I'm still your father and won't take anyone being disrespectful to me or who I'm seeing. Just like you two wouldn't want me to disrespect you or your girlfriends. Okay?"

When his sons only nodded their heads, Ryan strolled out of the barn. As he passed his two boys, he said, "I'll see you both later." He planned to try to see his daughter before he left. She was off that day, so she would be there the same time as Shannon. He just wanted to get this over with. Why don't they come to him? It wasn't like them.

As he got to the house, he could hear his daughter talking to Rosa. He hollered to get her attention. "Carly, can you come here?" Then he headed into his office.

Carly came into his office right after him, smiling. "Hey, Dad. What's up?" She gave him a hug and kiss on the cheek.

Damn, she's in a good mood and I'm about to ruin it. "Why weren't you nice to Shannon yesterday? And, no, Shannon hasn't said anything." He looked at his daughter to see the expression on her face. She looked upset, embarrassed, and pissed.

"I just don't think she's the right person for you. You need someone who has lived here and who knows everyone. I didn't say anything to her," Carly said in a very low voice.

"Have a seat." Ryan waved to the two chairs in front of his desk. Carly sat down, looking worried. "Out of you three kids, you took your mom's and my divorce the worst. What happened between us has nothing to do with you or your brothers. What's the real problem?"

Ryan watched as Carly took a deep breath and raised her tear filled eyes at him. "Why can't you and Mom date? Why can't you two find your way back together? My friend, Susan, her parents got back together after four years apart. I just want my parents together."

"I know you do, baby girl. But that's not going to happen. We are better people apart and neither of us regret the time we had together. Do you want to know why? Because we have three wonderful children, and I wouldn't change that." Ryan moved to pull his daughter into his arms and hugged her. He pulled back and wiped away a tear from her cheek. "I'm going to date. Either it will work with Shannon or not. Just like your mom dates. I hope she finds someone she can love, and I hope one day I can find love, too. Okay?"

His daughter didn't say anything and now had a guarded expression.

"You don't get a say, Carly. I'm going on a date, and you will be polite and respectful. Are we clear?" Ryan needed to get through to his daughter.

Carly only said two words. "Yes, sir." She made tracks to rejoin Rosa in the kitchen.

Ryan went upstairs to his bedroom to shower before he went to pick up Shannon. He really hoped his kids behaved and didn't embarrass him or make a scene. He finished and headed out the door. As he drove off he glanced at the rearview mirror and saw all three of his children on the porch, talking.

* * *

Shannon slept in, so when she got up she headed right into the shower to get ready for her first date with Ryan. It took her a little longer to get ready because she just had a hard time picking out what to wear. She wanted to look nice, but not too nice. Sexy but not sleazy. She just couldn't find a happy medium.

So she decided to just go with blue jeans and a white blouse with a cotton tank top underneath. When she finished getting dressed, she went back into the bathroom to finish her hair and put on a little makeup. She didn't want to wear too much, but she wanted to look nice.

Downstairs, she found Bianca and Lisa sitting on the couch, watching TV. "Hey. We thought we would have to get you up. You do know it's eleven-thirty and Ryan will be here any minute now." Lisa looked her over. "You look sexy. He won't know what hit him."

"I didn't want to look too nice, more relaxed and comfortable." Lisa knew how to make her nervous.

Bianca said with a smile, "You look great. Ignore Lisa. She's hoping to go to *After Hours*. We won't know until tonight." She got up to add, "I think she only wanted to see JP. She's been trying to find out what JP stands for. Do you know?"

"Oh, if you find out, you have to tell me. He won't tell, and I want to know. Hey, you can ask Ryan." Lisa was almost pleading.

"No, I don't know and, no, I'm not asking Ryan," Shannon stated firmly.

After about twenty-five minutes, Shannon got up to answer a knock at the door. Lisa shoved at her playfully as she passed her. Lisa cracked up. Shannon opened the door to let Ryan in and heard a noise behind her.

Smiling, he asked, "Hey, you ready?" At the same time, Erica came down the stairs looking tired and singing, "I hear you knocking but you can't come in," over and over.

Shannon just shook her head. "We go through this every morning. She sings a phrase of a song just to get on our nerves. What she doesn't know is that we think it's funny as shit." She picked up her purse and looked at her friends. "See ya later."

Ryan went to the passenger side of the truck and opened the door for her. When he got into the driver's side, he started the truck. "I hope you're hungry. Frank's Diner okay?"

"That sounds great and, yes, I'm hungry." She smiled at him.

They drove to the diner in a comfortable silence. She loved to look at the scenery. The mountains were beautiful. They looked like they were trying to reach the heavens. She liked to believe the clouds would stop to take a rest on the tops and then move on.

Before long, Ryan parked the truck in front of the diner. He hurried around to open the door for her. She found it really nice for someone to want to open doors for her. It hadn't happened to her in a very long time. Back home, not even when she would go out did a man entering or exiting a building hold the door open.

He offered his hand for Shannon to take so he could help her out of the truck. Slowly she placed her small hand into his large callused one and got out of the truck. When she got out, he never let go of her hand. They walked hand and hand to the diner. Ryan let go of her only to open the door, then guided her inside with his hand on her lower back.

Shannon could feel the heat from his palm on her back. Heat coursed through her, from her breasts and working its way down her abdomen. Before her thoughts got out of control, Nell came over with a smile.

EIGHT

Ryan felt her tense up then relax. He loved touching her, and the smell of her skin and hair made his cock hard every time. Thank God they were in public or he would move his hands under that t-shirt to her abdomen then to her breasts. Just when he started to fantasize about getting Shannon naked Nell came over, smiling.

"You want a table or booth?" Nell asked Ryan.

Ryan looked at Shannon to make sure, before asking, "Booth okay?"

"Sure." At that, Nell led them to the booth in the back.

They ordered drinks and Frank's special of

the day: bacon cheeseburger with fries and coleslaw. It was pleasant to sit down, just the two of them, and talk.

"When did you take over the ranch?" Shannon wanted to know more about the ranch. Okay, and him, too.

"My parents wanted to be young enough to travel when they retired, so when I turned...shit, I can't remember, it's been a long time. Twenty-six, maybe? They decided it was time to hand over the reins, so to speak. We had a lot more cattle when my parents ran the place. But, I love horses and have always been better with them than cattle."

"I notice you had Black Angus. How many head do you have?

"I have, at last count, twenty head. Like I said, I prefer horses to cattle. I have another barn about a mile in for the cattle. The hands, under the direction of Hank and my boys, take care of them. Dustin and Colby rotate who goes when they have to. I own the ranch, so I stay with the horses."

Shannon had to smile at the last comment. "Well, I'm with you there. Horses for me, not cattle. Sorry. What else does your ranch do?"

"In the winter, the lodge has a contract with me for sleigh rides and horseback riding by appointment. I have a hunting cabin for clients, or I rent it out for those who want to stay on a ranch. I bread my mares on a rotating schedule to give them time. And, of course, three of my males get requested for studding. Argo, the Appaloosa I just got, will be getting requests soon I'm sure."

"Argo? I didn't see him." He could see her trying to remember.

Before he could answer, Nell delivered their lunch. "Thanks, Nell. Argo stays in the far corral in the back with Missy. I won't let anyone ride him until I do. I ride all the new horses first, to get a feel for them."

Halfway through lunch, he finally asked the question that he really wanted her to answer. "Would you ever leave Florida? I mean, your daughter is in Maryland and your son is in Colorado."

She looked at him, really thinking about the question. "To be honest I never really thought about it, so I'm not sure how to answer that. Plus, my children never asked me to move."

Ryan could only nod his head. "Would you like to go out to the ranch and see Venus and her twins? We can go for a ride out to the lake again. This time, just the two of us." Ryan hoped the answer would be yes.

She didn't disappoint him. "That would be great."

Ryan held Shannon's hand and pointed things out on the way back to the ranch. He stopped halfway down his driveway and gestured as he explained what each building was for and explained his plans to add another building for storage. "I'm also thinking about building another hunting cabin. The one I have is always booked solid, and I have to turn down prospective renters. I'll need to figure out all the expenses first, to see if it's worth it. I hate accounting work."

"It's not really that hard, Ryan," Shannon replied.

Once he'd parked his truck, he walked around to get Shannon. This time she didn't wait for him and was halfway out of the truck by the time he came around. Taking her hand, he edged her over toward the barn to see the horses.

The horses were all in their stalls, getting ready to be fed. As they got inside, Shannon could smell the horses and hay. She could hear the beautiful animals stomping their hooves, making noises, and otherwise telling everyone they wanted to be fed or just wanted attention.

Ryan took her over to the first stall on the

right. Looking inside, Shannon saw Venus with her two little ones next to her. They were just adorable. One looked a lot like Venus, with brown with beige on her mane and front legs. The other one had some of Venus' looks, but must look more like the stallion who fathered her. She had a dark brown coat and only her mane matched the color of Venus.

As Ryan and Shannon moved deeper into the barn, Colby and Dustin came out of the storage room. Shannon remembered Ryan's explanation, that the barrels with the oat mix were essential to the horses' nutrition. The mixture contained oats, corn, and barley. They only gave them the oat mix once or twice a day, but the animals always needed more hay and clean water.

"Everything okay with the horses? Anything I need to know about?" Ryan asked his sons.

Colby was the first one to say anything. "Hi, Shannon. No, everything is good, Dad. We have to move Storm closer to Venus. He didn't like being separated from her. Your horse is being a pain in the fucking ass. Do you mind feeding him? He almost took off Dustin's head."

Shannon turned toward Colby. "Hi, Colby. It's nice to see you again."

Ryan shook his head and made his way down to Thunder's stall. "I got him. Why does he even try to take care of him?"

"Because we wanted to make sure he got fed. I know you would have, but I couldn't feed all the rest of them and not him." Dustin came out of the storage room with two buckets of water. He looked at Shannon. "Hello."

Smiling, Shannon responded, "Hello, Dustin."

Ryan handed Shannon a piece of apple to give to Thunder while he went to get the feed, hay, and water. When Ryan got back, Colby and Dustin just stood staring at Shannon. She reached inside the stall to give Thunder his treat. Thunder hung his head over the front of the stall door, letting Shannon stroke his head and neck.

Ryan walked over the her. "Back off, Thunder; you're going to get her blouse dirty."

"That's okay, big guy. He's gorgeous." Shannon looked at Ryan with a big smile.

As they headed out of the barn, Ryan introduced her to all the horses that she hadn't seen yet and took her outside to the corral. "This is my favorite place. The barn." He nodded to the barn. "People don't realize that horses have personalities just like us. Storm is the father of the twins, that's why he doesn't like being apart from Venus. He doesn't like the other males too close to her. But right now I can't have them in the same stall together."

Taking her around the property, he also showed Shannon the storage shed. The building stored a mower, four runners, two utility gators, and a bobcat and all kinds of tools attached to the side. "You call this a shed? What is that building next to it?" Ryan really had a great set-up.

"That building houses the horse trailer, wagon, and sled, along with anything needed to fix them and a cabinet with blankets. The garage for my truck is on the side of the house," he explained.

They walked around some more then headed back to the barn. The sun started to set. "What time is it?" Shannon asked.

"It's a little past six. Why? Have a curfew?" Ryan chuckled and moved before Shannon pushed him.

Shannon reached out to push him playfully but Ryan moved before she could. "Ha ha. Very funny. I didn't realize how late it is. It's just gone by fast, that's all."

They headed back into the barn with all the horses. "Want to take a ride?"

"Do you really have to ask me that?" She looked at him like it was a stupid question.

While he took care of Thunder, he asked his sons to saddle up Star Dust, a cremello Quarter Horse, and Snowy, a white half Paint horse and half Quarter Horse. After getting done and thanking his sons for getting the horses ready, Ryan handed Shannon the reins to Star Dust and he took Snowy and walked them up to the house.

Rosa met them on the porch with two saddlebags. "Thank you for doing this, Rosa. I know it's late. Have a great night. See you tomorrow." Ryan took the saddlebags from her and gave her a kiss on the cheek.

"You two have fun. Very nice to see you again, Shannon. Maybe next time Ryan will let us have some time to talk more than hello and goodbye," Rosa said, and then glanced at Ryan who just smiled at her.

They both mounted and Shannon followed Ryan. When she remembered the area, she asked, "Are we going to the lake?"

"Yes. I thought we could eat and watch the sunset," Ryan answered.

When they arrived, Ryan took care of the

horses first. A blanket lay on the dock with what looked like mason jars. When they got closer, Shannon noticed that the two mason jars were filled with sand and candles.

Ryan carried the two saddle bags and an extra rolled up blanket and began to pull everything out. Rosa had packed two sandwiches, pasta salad, two slices of pound cake, strawberries mixed with whipped cream, sweet tea, and wine.

After lighting all the candles, they sat down to eat what Rosa fixed.

"So, where are your parents? Do you have brothers or sisters?" Shannon asked before taking a bite of the pasta salad—it was so good. She needed to get the recipe from Rose.

"My parents and Steve's parents are in Colorado Springs. I have a sister, Rena. She's an artist and is being featured at the art gallery there. My parents go to all her openings. Do you have any siblings?"

"No, I'm an only child. My parents wanted more children, but I'm the only one. My parents still live in the same house I grew up in. I have a lot of friends there, still, and most of them also knew Tom. It's hard going back sometimes. It's just beautiful here." Shannon didn't want to talk about Tom.

Ryan seemed to take the hint that Shannon didn't want to talk about her deceased husband. He said, "Yes, it's beautiful. Because the lake is on my property, no one can use boats or jet skis. In the shed we have four canoes. I don't want to damage the lake. The snow from the mountains feeds into this lake, and that's why it's called Crystal Lake."

"So, the town is named after your lake? Why?" Shannon asked.

"Steve's and my ancestors are the founders of the town. But they wanted to preserve the lake, so my great-great...you know bought the property around it to make sure it stayed that way. We do have town functions here and everyone knows they are more than welcome to come here, but no cars or trucks. So, they come up to the main house and we load everyone in the wagon."

"That is extremely smart." Shannon was impressed.

Before long, a full moon started to rise and the stars would be twinkling in the sky. They both leaning back on their elbows. Ryan leaned in with his hand to place a lock of hair behind her ear. "I enjoy being with you, Shannon. Maybe we can do something together tomorrow."

Shannon blushed. "I'd like that."

Ryan lowered his head, his lips hovering just above hers, seeming to want to give her a chance to pull back. However, instead, she moved forward. She whispered his name against his lips right before Ryan sucked her bottom lip into his month then crushed his lips to hers and deepened the kiss. He tasted of the strawberries that they'd eaten. He had his own unique taste and it was addictive. She wanted more.

He followed her down as she lay down on the blanket. Ryan half lay down next to her, one elbow by her head and the other hand on her waist. His tongue explored her mouth. Ryan couldn't stop himself; his hand moved slowly from her waist to her rib cage so his thumb was right underneath her breast.

Shannon fired Ryan up and he was only kissing her. Moving his hand to right underneath her breast, her breathing came out deeper and heavier.

He felt one of her hands grip the back of his shirt and tried to pull him closer. Her other hand moved up to his biceps to his shoulder then to the back of his neck to deepen the kiss. He loved how she tried to take over the kiss. He was naturally demanding, dominating, and passionate.

She broke the kiss for needed air. She

hadn't felt like this for years. She tilted her head to give him better access to her ear and neck. Then his mouth finally moved to her ear and he sucked her earlobe into his mouth. Breathing just as hard as Shannon, he whispered into her ear, "Shannon, you need to tell me now if you want to me to stop. I won't be able to if we go any further." He looked into her eyes. "I want you more than I've ever wanted anyone, and I mean anyone. Tell me, Shannon, do you want me? Or should we stop? I'm willing to wait. You're worth it."

"Will anyone come out here?" Shannon didn't want his children to come out to find them naked together.

With a smile, he said, "Come with me." She could only nod. Leaning down, he placed a quiet kiss on her lips and forehead. They got up gathered everything up and took the candles with them.

As they headed in the direction of the shed, she asked, "Ryan, we aren't going into the shed, are we?"

"No, look just past the shed," Ryan assured her.

"You had this planned." She wanted to die on the spot.

"No, of course not. The boys set this up

yesterday to air it out for a camping trip they have planned," Ryan explained. Relief washed over her face. "Shannon, I didn't plan anything happening. Yes, I set up the food and blanket to watch the sunset. We don't have to do anything you don't want to. I'll be happy just holding you, kissing you, and maybe getting to second base." The last part was said with a chuckle and a wink.

When they got to the tent, Ryan blew out the candles and set them down. Taking her hand, he led her inside. She eyed the camping equipment on one side of the tent and spotted the battery operated lantern. Ryan sat down and Shannon straddled his lap. This would give him access to not only her neck, but her breasts as well.

Ryan slid his hands under her blouse, over her ribs to her breasts at the same time she had her fingers in his hair and kissed him like her life depended on this kiss. His hands squeezed her full, round breasts, and she loved the feel of his touch. He moved this thumbs over her hard nipples over her bra, and that had her rocking against him.

He moved her blouse up to her breasts, over her head, and then unhooked her bra. The straps moved down her arms and fell away. He sucked in a breath. "You are beautiful."

He kissed her breastbone and dragged open mouthed kisses across her right breast. Shannon could feel his hand on the center of her back while the other squeezed her left breast. She held onto his shoulders, her nails digging in.

She started to gather up his shirt, needing to feel him skin to skin. She could feel the ragged scars on him. "I love the feel of your skin. I haven't been with anyone like this for a long time." His skin rippled at her touch. She wanted to know what his skin tasted like. She planned on finding out.

"You make me feel like I'm a teenager finding love for the first time." Just then he slowly moved the zipper down on her jeans. Looking down into his eyes, she could see the raw sexual heat in his gaze. Ryan helped her to stand and slowly lowered her jeans and lace panties at the same time. "Fuck, you're absolutely gorgeous."

Her breath hitched when Ryan went to his knees and placed kisses on top of her shaved mound. Shannon parted her legs to give him better access. She opened her mouth, to gasp, "Ryan…" She couldn't get anything else out.

Shannon backed up and encouraged Ryan to stand. Lowing his zipper, she pushed his jeans down and her eyes widened. "Is that a good look or bad look? I'm hoping good," Ryan asked as he placed a kiss on her forehead.

Needing to touch him, Shannon cupped him and massaged him until he rocked hard against her.

Grabbing her wrists, he held them behind her and together. "I won't last if you keep touching me. But, I am going to taste you." He knelt, taking a nipple into his mouth, and sucked.

His hand roamed down to her heat and he curled one finger inside slowly, then added another. Moving his fingers in and out slowly, he scissored them ever so slightly. Ryan let go of her hand, moving to her ass. "Lay down, Shannon."

Instead of doing what he asked, she started moving her hips against his hand. "Oh, God. Ryan...I can't wait. Please, don't stop." She felt her body start tightening on his fingers and then the tingle down her spine. Ryan pulling his fingers out right before she came. "Nooooo."

"Lie down, Shannon. I'll take care of you, but I want you to lie down." He helped her to lie down on the blanket. Ryan quickly placed their clothes aside and folded the sleeping bag in half for Shannon's head. He spread her legs wide so he could settle between them.

Her folds were wet, pink, and swollen with need. Shannon raised her hips on her own, wanting him to touch her again. Ryan moved his hands to her folds. "Please." He spread her with one hand; at the same time, he slid his two fingers back inside and started moving them. Her hips moved up and down, wanting more, but they stilled when he sucked her clit between his teeth. As soon as he nipped her clit, Shannon lost it. She legs spread wider as her pussy clamped down on his fingers, trying to suck them in deeper, and she pushed hard against his hand. Ryan looked up, wanting to see her face and the passion as she came for him. He kept pumping his fingers and curling them inside to hit her g-spot every time.

As she came down from her high, Ryan sat up. His one hand cupped her and his other hand squeezed the base of his cock. He had his eyes closed and Shannon wanted to touch him. The purple head of his cock look painful. As she moved to her elbows, he growled, "Don't move, Shannon. I just need a minute." His voice sounded so deep and rough, she could feel herself getting wetter, and rubbed herself against his hand. "Shannon, be still."

"I can't. Come to me, Ryan. I need you inside." She has never felt so needy before, not even during her marriage. It was almost painful for her

Noticing him reaching for his jeans, she raised an eyebrow at him. "Condom."

He opened it with his teeth and slid it down his shaft. Leaning on one elbow, he guided his cock to her opening. As he slid in, both of them sighed. "Fuck. You feel so good. Hot." He moved in without stopping until he was balls deep. Then he started moving, slow and deep. They kissed roughly, her hand on his back, meeting his thrust. He lifted one of her legs and placed it around his waist. His thrusts became faster and harder. She was so damn close. Reaching down between them with his other hand, he found her clit and rubbed hard and pinched. She came again with a scream, and he followed right behind her.

Ryan leaned down on his elbows and kissed each cheek, forehead, and then her lips. Rolling to his side, he pulled Shannon into his chest. She rested her head on him as his arms came around her. "I didn't plan on this. I'm normally not like this."

"Like what?" He smiled as he moved his hand down to her ass then up to her hip.

She playfully slapped at his chest and smiled. "You know what I meant."

Chucking out loud, he replied, "Yes, I know. For the record, I'm not either. I haven't been with anyone since my...for a long time." Relief washed over her when he didn't finish that thought. Shannon felt so relaxed in his arms and didn't want to ruin the moment. "Stay out here with me tonight."

Placing her chin on his chest and looking into his blue-grey eyes, she said, "Yes."

* * *

Ryan sat up and pulled the other blanket over them. Shannon's breathing became even, telling him that she already was falling asleep, probably from exhaustion. Relaxing, he tightened his arms and closed his eyes.

Ryan woke up hearing noises outside. Grabbing his jeans, he rushed out of the tent to see who came so early in the morning. His saw his son, Dustin. "What are you doing here?" He didn't want Shannon to wake up and hear someone, so he walked over to him.

Dustin looked at the tent. "Carly came over, wanting to know if we knew where you are. I said I would check at the lake. I didn't hear you drive Shannon back." He was clearly fishing for information.

"That's none of your business. You can go back to the house or barn." Ryan crossed his arms, but his son didn't move.

"Don't you think you're moving too fast here? You've only been divorced from Mom for a little over three years," Dustin asked his father, without anger in his voice, but in confusion.

Ryan didn't understand the problem. "The three of you wanted me to get out and I did. Your mom has been dating for years, and you guys are fine with that, but you have a problem with me."

"Go out, yes. With Steve or JP. Not go out and hook up," Dustin said in a raised voice.

He moved closer to his son and looked down. "Boy, you better watch your damn mouth. That is what is called a fucking double standard, and I won't stand for it. Why didn't you say anything earlier? You will not start here, knowing there's a chance of Shannon overhearing. Get your ass back to the barn or we can talk about who you're dating. Choose."

Looking at the stunned look on his face, he watched Dustin finally dart back to his horse and ride off. *Damn Vicky*. She needed to tell the kids that she got engaged seven months ago and would be getting remarried soon. But, no she didn't want her kids upset so she had been putting it off. Maybe Ryan wouldn't be having such a hard time if his ex would just tell them.

Ryan had been on a trip to look at two horses he considered buying when he saw Vicky and Pete at the restaurant. He attempted to sneak out until she saw him. She introduced them and then informed him they were celebrating their engagement. They all ended up eating together. The two of them were a perfect match. They both loved living in the city, travel, and parties. He loved the quiet life, horses, mountains, small towns, and the wildlife around him. Vicky made him promise not to say anything to their kids yet. It's been seven fucking months and still she hadn't said anything. Damn, he might have to inform them if this kept up.

After he saddled up the horses he went to the tent to wake Shannon. "Wake up, sunshine." He kissed her forehead.

Ryan got everything together and cleaned up. Shannon helped him finish after getting dressed. They rode back in silence and it gave him time to think.

From the look on her face, Ryan could tell she was deep in thought. God, he hoped she didn't regret last night. How could he feel this strongly for someone so fast? It felt right and he had a feeling she was going to fight this.

His kids seemed to have a problem, well, not Colby.

NINE

Getting back to the barn Ryan and Shannon took the saddles off the horses, brushed them down, fed them, and gave them water. Colby came over and offered to take Star Dust from her.

"Thank you for asking, Colby, but I've got it."

Dustin didn't say anything and barely looked at her. Carly stood on the porch when they left the barn and went to Ryan's truck.

Ryan reach across the seat for Shannon's hand and rubbed his thumb across her knuckle. As they drove, she looked down at their hands, and said, "You've been really quiet. Is there a problem that I need to know about? Or do you regret last night?" Her heart started to sink, worried about the response she might get.

The truck pushed off the road and before she could say anything, Ryan got out and strolled to her side. *Shit, this is bad.* He opened the door and turned her sideways.

Ryan took her hands. "Shannon, I don't regret last night. Do you?" His hand had moved to her hips in order to move her closer.

"No. You just seem distant or maybe upset. Does it have to do with any feelings you have for your ex-wife? I just don't want to be someone used to upset an ex." She felt like shit saying this, but she believed in being honest and not holding back. Plus, Ryan got under her shield and broke it down, and that scared the shit out of her.

Ryan didn't realize that his silence would mean anything. But he had been quiet and had held off touching her until they got into the truck. "No, I have no feelings for Vicky, and we don't want each other anymore. I just don't know what's wrong with my kids. I'm sorry if I made you feel bad." He seemed nervous. "I really like you and want to spend more time with you. I want to see you later today. What do you say?"

"I would like that. But I don't want to upset our kids." Shannon wouldn't be the reason for Ryan's kids being upset with him. She would stop seeing him.

He placed his hands on her face and kissed her long. "Good. I'll text you later. I need to get you back to your friends, or I'm going to take you right here. Don't you worry about my kids. I'll talk to them." With that said, he got back into the truck.

Ryan went to the front door with Shannon. She didn't know what to do. "So, I'll hear from you later, right?" She sounded clingy.

"Yes. Maybe dinner? This way you can spend time with your friends." Moving closer, he placed his hand on her waist.

Moving her hand to his chest, she agreed, "Dinner." Ryan captured her month in a kiss that made her go weak in the knees. He released her and placed a kiss on her forehead and headed to his truck.

Shannon watched Ryan drive off before going into the cabin to face her friends. The three of them looked amused. "Not a damn word."

"Not going to say that you never made it back or that you're wearing the same clothes from last night. Not going to say a thing." *Lisa, such a smart ass*.

"We take it you enjoyed yourself." Erica just chuckled as a pillow came flying at her from Bianca.

She sat next to Lisa. "Wonderful. I had so much fun. Oh, the babies are so cute."

"You're falling for him. Aren't you?" Lisa looked concerned.

Shannon wasn't sure what to say. But the ringing of cell phone saved her. It couldn't be Ryan already. When she looked at the screen. "It's Dylan." She got up to answer the call. "Hey, sweetie. How are you?"

"Just wanted to check in while I can. I've been really busy. How's the vacation?" She hesitated, not sure what to say and how much to tell him. "Mom, what's going on?"

"Nothing bad. I-I met someone." *Silence. Okay.* "His name is Ryan and he owns a horse ranch. He has twin sons, Dustin and Colby, and a daughter, Carly. We have a lot in common and enjoy the same things. I enjoy being around him."

"Who are you trying to convince, me or you?" Her son listened too well.

Taking a deep breath, she tried again. "No one. Just nervous telling my son. I really like him; I think you two would like him, too. But his kids seem to be a problem. You know I don't want to be the reason for tension within his family." Shannon went on, telling her son about the county fair, *After Hours*, the horseback riding, and yesterday… leaving out the sex, of course.

"Sounds like you more than like him. If you're asking would I be okay with this, the answer is yes, as long as he understands he will never replace Dad. But I want you happy; you're too young to be alone." Her son was very special.

They talked some more about Montana, Ryan, and he even asked if she would be moving to be with him. That question, she would have to think about. She didn't even know if Ryan would want her to stay with him.

She came back into the cabin and told her friends about the phone call. None of them looked surprised. "So, what are you going to do now?" Bianca leaned in.

"To be honest, I would stay with him. How can I feel so much for someone in a short amount of time? We haven't discussed what either one of us wants. Yes, we want to see each other, and we like one another, but is it too soon?" Shannon stared moving toward the stairs and then the shower. "I'm heading upstairs. Would you all have a problem if I see him today, too?"

"Of course not. The three of us made plans already." Erica must have had more than a single cup of coffee already. She bounced on the balls of her feet.

* * *

Dylan hung up with his mother and called his sister, Alexis. "What's up, big brother?" She sounded way too happy.

"You're in a fantastic mood. Everything good, I take it?" Dylan loved talking to his sister. She never held back and said exactly what she meant without editing the words.

"Awww, I love when you call, trying to act like you want to just chat when you really have something on your mind. So, what the hell is going on?"

"I just got off the phone with Mom. Have you talked to her?" First, he wanted to know if she knew about Ryan.

Alexis sounded worried. "No, she called me but I had to take my final. I did send a text and everything was good at the time. For now, I'm done with school. Is she okay?"

"Yes, she's good. Well, really good. She met someone. His name is Ryan." Dylan went on and told his sister everything that he knew. "She really likes this guy. I can tell by the way she talks about him."

"How do you feel about that? Me, I'm glad to be honest. She should live again and love again." His sister, the hopeless romantic.

"I'm good. I'll go out there to see her and meet this guy. You going to show up? I'll bet you twenty bucks I beat you there." She wasn't going to fall for it.

"Oh, you are on. You forget school is out and I can take off any time. You have to ask and go through how many channels? I'll see you there." She hung up on her brother and started to make arrangements to head out to Montana.

* * *

When Ryan got back to the ranch, he went into the barn to check on Venus. "How are you doing, girl? Taking care of your babies?" Venus hung her head over the corner and nudged his hand. Rubbing her nose, Ryan felt a nudge to his shoulder. "Storm, I'm not hurting her." Damn, the horse was protective of Venus.

Across from Storm, a loud snort and stomping could be heard. Argo, his new Quarter Horse, didn't like being ignored. "So, you're going to be just as demanding as Thunder. Maybe I'll take you out for a run soon. What do you say, boy?" Argo started moving his head up and down, and stomped his hoof in agreement.

Ryan stayed in the barn, checking on all the horses. Shannon would love this. He wanted to share his world and life with someone, and Shannon was what his heart wanted. Could he really have a woman in his life again?

Three hours later, Ryan headed up to house to shower and change. When he walked upstairs, he could hear his daughter on the phone. "Mom, will you please call me? I really need to talk to you. This is important."

Leaning again the doorframe, he asked, "Does your need to talk to your mother have anything to do with me?" Ryan glanced at his daughter.

Carly must have thought she'd closed her door. "Um, no. I just need to talk to Mom, is all."

"Hmm, you don't really think that I believe that, do you? I'm not sure what problem you have with Shannon, but I'm going to tell you the same thing I told Dustin this morning. It's none of your business, your brothers', or your mother's business. We talked earlier. You need to talk to me about this, not your mother."

Carly looked down and whispered, "Yes, sir. I understand." Ryan could tell she really didn't. He was going to have to call Vicky himself.

"If you keep this up, I'll be taking your phone from you for a week. And, yes, I can. I paid for the phone and I pay the damn bill." With that, Ryan turned and headed to his bedroom.

Rosa stood by the hope chest with his laundry. "I think she still believes that you and Vicky will get back together. You may want to let them know about the engagement."

Ryan turned around, "How...? Never mind; I stopped trying to figure out how you find shit out. I know, about Vicky... I might have to tell them. The reason she isn't answering her phone is because they're on some cruise again for three weeks. She told the kids they're in Vegas."

"Yes, the Hawaiian cruise. I know." Rosa handed him a towel. "Are you going to see Shannon again today? She is good for you. You are living again and not spending sun up to sun down out in the barn or in the field."

Ryan just shook his head, "I don't want to know how you know so much or where you get your information. Do you think I'm going too fast? I'll admit I'm falling for her hard. I love being around her... we have so much in common and enjoy the same things. What do you think, Rosa?"

She came up to Ryan patted his cheek. "It's up to you. I will only say this: Listen and follow your heart. That will never fail you. If Shannon is what you want, then tell her and get her to stay." After that, she left his room. *That is one amazing woman.*

Ryan got clean clothes and went into his bathroom to shower. He wanted to get back to Shannon. Maybe take her to dinner at the Blackfoot Lodge and hike one of the trails. He needed to talk to her about her plans. She would love the scenery there. He noticed Shannon taking a lot a pictures, but he'd bet none of them have her in them. He remembered her telling him that her daughter was taking photography classes. She might send her the pictures.

He walked into the kitchen to find Rosa preparing for dinner. "I'm going to take Shannon to the Lodge for dinner. So, it will only be the kids."

"Well, you have fun. Just remember, their cooking isn't as good as mine. Don't forget to tell Shannon that." Ryan kissed her on the cheek, stealing a handful of raw carrots. Rosa playfully slapped at him. "You are going to ruin your dinner," she called out to him right before he closed the door.

Sending a text to Shannon, he let her know

that he would be taking her out to dinner. He noticed Colby by his truck. Damn, now he would be late. "Son."

"You going out again?" Colby just wanted to find out why his brother was acting like an asshole.

Ryan looked at his son, really looked. He had no emotion on his face. "Yes, I'm taking Shannon up to Blackfoot Lodge for dinner. Do you need something before I leave?"

Colby shoved his hand through his hair. "No, not really. Just wondering if you know what's wrong with Dustin. He's been an ass all damn morning and afternoon."

Figures. "Let's just say he didn't like that I don't have to answer his questions and told him it's not his fucking business."

"Okay, that's why." Colby didn't seem surprised to Ryan.

"Do you have a problem with me seeing Shannon?" Ryan might as well find out now.

Colby seemed shocked. "No. She seems nice, and you can tell that she loves horses. I'm glad you're getting out, Dad. I know that Mom has been dating for years. It's nice to see you going out, living your life with someone you obviously enjoy being around. I'm happy for you. It's the other two, not me."

Ryan was glad that one of his kids didn't have a problem with his living again and dating. "Thanks. I'm late; gotta go. See you sometime tomorrow." He started to open his truck door, then added, "If you wouldn't mind, could you talk to your brother and sister for me? Maybe they'll listen to you."

His son seemed to consider his request. "I'll try," he said finally.

"That's all I ask." Then Ryan left to see the one person he couldn't wait to see again.

* * *

When Ryan pulled up to the cabin, Shannon walked out. "I would've come to the door to get you." He gave her a quick kiss.

"I know, but the girls left already to go out." She got into the truck when Ryan opened the door.

Ryan headed to Blackfoot Lodge. She looked puzzled, so he figured he'd explain where they were going. "I thought we could have an early dinner at the Lodge and then take a walk on one of the trails?"

"Great. I actually have been looking forward to seeing the Lodge up close."

The drive went by fast and, before long, they parked and headed up to the Lodge. Ryan asked for the corner booth in the back to give them some privacy. "Rosa wanted me to tell you that the food here isn't as good as hers. I think she's hoping we would be eating at my place."

"She's not upset, is she? I don't want to offend her," Shannon said.

Just then, the waitress came over. "Good evening, Mr. Collins. How is Missy? I hope I can come back and ride her again."

"Why don't you call the office number and let us know when? Shannon, I'm sorry, this is Stacey. She went to school with my sons. Stacey, Shannon Ward," Ryan stated.

"What would you like to drink?" She took their drink orders and left to fill them.

"You said you worked in a bank, in accounting. What exactly does that entail?" He hoped he could come up with something local for her or even have her work for him. He hated doing his accounting books for the ranch.

"In a nutshell? We keep the general ledger accounts balanced. I only want to do accounting. At one time I tried to find another job, but nothing came of it," Shannon explained.

Their dinner came—steak, twice-baked potato, and mixed medley. Ryan wanted to talk to her about staying over dinner. But every time he wanted to bring it up, his nerves got the best of him and he chickened out. They skipped dessert and went for a short hike on one of the trails.

Stopping at one point, he showed her a Mule deer with its young. Shannon got out her camera and snapped some pictures. "They have bigger ears than deer in Maryland."

"They sure do. Beautiful." Ryan looked at Shannon when he said that, not the deer.

Ryan turned her around. "We need to head back. It's going to be getting dark soon."

Walking back to the truck about an hour later, they both decided they were ready for dessert. They headed back to Ryan's, knowing that Rosa made strawberry shortcake. He wanted Shannon in his house, hopefully for good one day. He still struggled with how to talk to Shannon about staying.

They rode back in a comfortable silence, enjoying being with one another. He pulled up to the front of his house and led her inside. In the kitchen he got out two plates, cutting two slices of cake. They sat at the small table together.

He took Shannon's hand and led her to the family room where he turned on the radio, setting a timer so it would turn off in two hours. "Dance with me?" he requested. They danced, and laughed when something fast came on and they tried to keep up. Shannon laughed harder whenever he missed and stepped on her foot.

At one point Ryan picked her up and danced her around the room with her off her feet. Ryan caught his sons looking through the window, but didn't acknowledge that he saw them. They were having just too much fun.

When a slow song finally came back on, he placed her back on her feet. Both of them breathed heavily and their hearts pounded. He ran his hand under her shirt up her back while inhaling her. *God, he loved the smell of her shampoo: coconut.*

Turning her around, he wrapped his arms around her, pressing his hard cock against her lower back. "Come upstairs with me. Stay the night."

"What about your daughter?" Shannon asked.

"She's spending the night at a friend's house. Rosa left a note on the refrigerator door." He slowly moved her toward the stairs.

Taking her hand, he said, "Shannon, I want to take you upstairs and make love to you.

Please tell me you want this, too?"

"Yes" was all she said, and they started up the stairs.

His bedroom looked more like a suite, and it featured a California king in the middle of the room with a hope chest at the end of the bed. Two dressers were on each side and a forty-inch television hung on the wall. The colors of his bedroom were mostly earth tones with some blues.

He crushed his mouth to Shannon's before she could consider his personal space further. Moving his mouth from her jaw to neck, he slipped his hand to her ass and lifted her up as he hurried to the side of the bed. Sitting her on the side, he slowly slid her shirt up to bare her full breasts. "Arms up." He took her blouse off and placed open-mouth kisses between her breasts while unhooking her bra. He watched as the straps fell down her arms to bare her to his gaze.

His hand stroked down the front of her jeans to find her clit, and circled the hard nub. "Ryan, please. I want to feel your skin, too." Her hips rocked against his hand as he touched her.

Pulling back, she took off his shirt. While Ryan took off his jeans, she stood to take hers off, too. He backed her up and placed her on the edge of the bed. He slid down her body, leaving open-mouthed kisses as he went. Every cell in her body erupted with need for Ryan.

His hand went down and slid one finger inside and found her already wet and ready. With the other hand he reached inside the night stand and took out a condom and placed it on the bed. He added a second finger and moved them into her damp heat. "Come for me, Shannon."

Two more strokes and she shattered, screaming his name. "Ryan!"

Standing, Ryan opened the package, slipped the condom down his shaft, and guided his cock to her opening. He surged inside in one thrust. Ryan only had one thought. *Heaven.* "I can't go slow."

She clutched and gripped him so tight he wouldn't last long anyway.

"Take me, Ryan." Tilting her hips up to go deeper he thrust in and out fast, hard and rough. She fisted his comforter in her hand, her knuckles turning white. Ryan held her hips so tight that there would be bruises later.

Every inch of his body craved her. Tightening around him even more, he knew she teetered on the edge again. Ryan could tell she's holding off. "With me, Shannon."

"Not yet." Wrapping her legs around his thighs, Shannon rolled Ryan to his back. Ryan ran his hands over her smooth skin. Groaning as she worked her entrance over his shaft, she lowered herself. She rode up and down with her nails scoring his chest. Ryan was so aroused he was losing his mind, and he madly thrusted upward.

"Fuck. Faster, baby." Ryan felt his balls draw up and the tingling running down his spine. After two hard trusts he came hard. Shannon slammed down one last time as her legs gripped his hips. Throwing her head back, her inner muscle tightened around Ryan even more and she screamed.

With him still inside of her, she rested her head on his shoulder. "You falling asleep on me?" Ryan asked as he ran his hands down her back to her ass and squeezed.

"No," Shannon said, a little breathless.

Ryan slowly rolled them to the side, removed the condom, and put it in the trash can. Going back to the bed, he picked her up and took her into the bathroom. Placing her on her feet, he turned on the shower.

They took turns washing each other. Ryan's desire started to stir again with her hands on him. After drying off, they headed back to the bedroom. Pulling the covers back, Shannon lay down in the middle of the bed and Ryan climbed in with her. As he tugged her into his arms, she looked up at him. "I had a great day and an even better evening." She said the last part with a smile.

"Well, I enjoyed myself, too. Maybe we can do it again. Just give me an hour to rest. I'm not as young as I used to be." Ryan smiled back at her.

Moving his hand up and down her back, he whispered, "Go to sleep. I'll wake you up in a good way or you can wake me."

With that Shannon closed her eyes and fell into a relaxing sleep.

TEN

Ryan turned his head and looked at the most beautiful sight he had ever seen— *Shannon*. They'd made love repeatedly, all night and into the early morning hours. Shannon rested her head on his chest, their legs intertwined as they held onto each other. He lay there, content until the one thought from the back of his mind entered. *Shannon is due to leave in four days.*

Ryan needed to talk to her at breakfast about staying with him. His heart ached at the thought of Shannon leaving. He wanted her to stay, to make a new life with him in Montana. They could love each other with all their hearts and souls, for she had penetrated his heart and he could feel her imbedded in his soul. *I can't let her go; I want a life with her. But does she love me just as much? If she did, would she be willing to stay here with me?*

He knew he should get up and get started with the chores that needed to be done, but he just couldn't make himself leave the woman next to him. The sun had just started to come through the curtains in his bedroom. *The day is going to be beautiful.* Just then, Shannon stretched and moaned. "Good morning, sleepy head."

She looked up and grinned. "Good morning. What time is it?" She raised her hand to the center of Ryan's chest; he loved the feel of her hands on him. How long could they stay in bed and not move?

"It's early, about five in the morning. I probably need to get up and help my boys with the chores. But first I have something to take care of…" That's when he rolled Shannon onto her back and lowered his lips to hers. Kissing her deeply, his tongue danced with hers. One hand grazed her breast to rub her nipple with his thumb and forefinger. Getting on his knees, Ryan spread her thighs open to lay completely between them.

Her whimpers made his cock harder by the minute as her pussy became wet. "You are so beautiful. I love seeing you like this, so aroused," Ryan whispered into her ear then trailed kisses down her neck to her collarbone.

She arched her back. "Ryan, please." She

put her hands in his hair to push him lower. His mouth was now level with her breast.

"I know. But not yet. I want you to come first. Then I'm going to take you hard and fast. I can't go slow and don't want to. Both of us need this too much." Ryan then took her nipple into his mouth and sucked hard. Lapping the hard peak and nipping at it gave her the right amount of pain; then licking it turned it into pleasure. The other hand left her other nipple and slowly journeyed to her stomach, and then her shaven mound. He found her wet clit hard and pushing out from its hood. Knowing it would not take much to make her go over the edge, he started to rub his fingers over the lips of her pussy and slid his middle finger inside. Her inner muscles gripped his finger and tried to suck it in deeper. However, he just left it inside, only moving it in circles every so often. He wanted to get her mindless.

Shannon rocked her hips up, trying to get his finger deeper into her sex. *She's so close.* With his hand on her pussy, a finger inside, and his mouth on her breast, he knew he drove her closer and closer to the edge. "Ryan, now," she pleaded as her fingers dug into him.

Ryan knew how badly she needed to come. He slowly released her breast and moved down her body, placing his month on her skin as he went. Shannon's breathing became faster as she tried to get him to move the finger that stilled inside her. He moved completely between her thighs and spread them wider, his hand wet from Shannon's juices. Keeping his eyes on her, he breathed, smelling how aroused she was. He leaned forward and lightly licked her from his finger to her clit. "Mmm, your taste drives me crazy, honey." Her mouth opened in a silent cry. He knew he couldn't hold her off much longer.

He started to thrust his finger in and out in a slow, steady rhythm and added a second finger. Keeping his eyes on Shannon, he sucked her clit into his mouth at the same time he moved his fingers faster. Shannon's legs shook and tightened on his arms. She clamped down around Ryan's fingers and shattered as he curved them to rub her g-shot.

Ryan moved up her body and kissed Shannon. "You are so beautiful, Shannon. I love how your body comes alive for me." She nodded her head. Her hands grazed up his arms to his shoulders and around his neck. Shannon pulled his face down toward her and whispered, "I need you just as bad, Ryan."

That's all it took for Ryan to slam home. Taking Shannon's mouth in a heated kiss, he put all his emotion into it and hoped she would understand just how much he needed and wanted her. When he released her mouth, they both gasped for air. Ryan entwined their fingers above her head and thrusted fast and deep. Shannon met his thrust with one of her own, wrapping her legs around his waist.

Ryan had never felt so much pleasure at one time, like coming home. "You feel so good, baby. I want to be in you forever." He started to slowly withdraw and then drove into her, wanting to feel her inner muscles squeeze him back inside.

When Shannon started to whimper, Ryan released her hands and shifted one hand to squeeze her breast. He took her nipple into his mouth and sucked hard as she arched her back. He stilled inside her as she came again, feeling her inner muscles clamp down on him like a vise. The need to come almost took over, but he didn't want this to end yet. He moved to the other nipple and sucked that one into his mouth, but used his teeth to nip at the hard bud. Shannon arched her back and came for the third time. *God, she feels so good around me.*

He released her nipple with one last nip then licked the sting away. He eased up onto his weakened knees, ran his hands from her breasts over her ribs, and gripped her hips. Shannon tried to get Ryan to move but he just glanced at her.

He looked down at where they joined together. As he slowly withdrew, her juices ran down between them to her forbidden hole. He withdrew himself from her sex, gripped his cock in his hand, and slid himself between her cheeks. He made sure to rub the head over her hole. She moved her legs without him guiding her wider and up. He felt her moving with him. Gently he moved her right leg up to his shoulder; this gave him better access to her ass.

She stilled when Ryan not only slid himself back into her but also moved one of his fingers to rub her own juices around her hole. Ryan met Shannon's gaze, "Have you ever been taken here?" As he asked, he slowly pushed one finger into her ass and moved it in and out slowly.

Shannon tried to move to get him to go deeper. He pushed a second finger inside her hole and started to scissor his fingers. Shannon pushed back. "I wanted to, but never did. To…"

"It's okay." Ryan knew by the look on her face that it upset her, almost saying his name. "I just want to get you ready. Tell me now if I need to stop and not go any further." He didn't stop moving his fingers in her hole, but kept his cock still inside of her pussy. When she said nothing and just pushed back against his fingers, he knew she was ready.

Ryan removed his finger, gripped the base of his shaft, and squeezed, which gave him a minute to get his control back. With the other hand, he slid his thumb inside and laid his palm against her clit, not putting too much pressure on hard little bud. Going slow to give her time to change her mind, he moved himself to her ass. He carefully pushed in then backed out and pushed even further. Shannon started to tense up, but Ryan put pressure on her clit and moved his thumb in circles inside her.

"Baby, push out as I push in. Try to relax your muscles." Ryan guided her through, knowing she would be nervous, aroused, and scared. He could feel her pushing out and he took that moment to push the rest of the way inside at a slow, steady rate.

"Shannon, you okay?" Before Ryan moved, he would ensure she was okay. She felt so amazing and tight. Shannon looked up at him with so much passion in her eyes that Ryan almost lost all sense of control. All he wanted to do the take her hard.

"Ryan." She glanced at him over her shoulder. "It feels good and hurts a little."

"Can I move? I'll go slow," Ryan asked as he continued to move his thumb inside her and pressed harder on her clit. He really needed to move. He could feel himself flexing into her ass as she tightened more around him.

He moaned loudly when her ass squeezed his cock harder than before. "Shit!" He tried to push in more as she gripped his shaft. He felt like his cock got larger and it was beginning to feel painful. He needed to move and come. If he didn't move soon he was going to lose control and end up hurting her.

Getting a slight nod, he started moving. He looked down to watch himself moving in and out of her ass. *That is one of the sexist things I've ever seen.* More of her juices ran out of her as he moved his thumb in time with the thrusting in her ass. When he felt the tingling start running down his spine, he pinched her clit and moved faster. Shannon exploded and clamped down around his cock. Two strokes later, come shot out into her ass so hard he thought he might pass out from the pleasure. He released her clit and shoved two fingers into her sex.

Ryan eased out of Shannon's ass and got up to get something to clean them both up. Shannon's eyes flew open when she felt something warm on her sex and ass. Her pussy swollen and sensitive, she let out a moan when Ryan cleaned her up.

Ryan pulled her to him, and she sighed. "Go to sleep, baby." *I love you,* Ryan so wanted to say, but held back. What would she say if he said those three words out loud? Would she say them back, or deny her own feelings for him? Bianca said that Shannon might fight her feelings for him because she thought she was betraying her late husband. He admired her loyalty and devotion. *How do I convince her that, just like me, she deserves to find love again? I'm going to talk to her. I have to… we only have four more days together. This can't wait anymore. I just hope she's willing to stay, and loves me just as much as I love her.*

With that last thought Ryan pulled Shannon even closer, their limbs intertwined, and fell into a peaceful sleep.

ELEVEN

Ryan woke up hearing his stomach growling. As he turned to look at the clock, he heard and felt Shannon laughing. "Just what are you laughing at?" *Shit, it's eight.*

"You. Your stomach woke me up." For some reason, that made her laugh even harder.

That's when he rolled Shannon to her stomach and started to rub her back and tickle her at the same time. "Now you have a good reason to laugh, you imp." He kissed his way down her spine until he reached her ass, and kissed each cheek. He knew she would most likely be sore, only having anal sex this morning for the first time. Nipping her butt cheeks, he asked, "Why don't we continue this in the shower?"

He smacked her ass and headed to the

bathroom. Shannon jumped off the bed, hot on his heels, laughing.

Ryan then went to the shower, turned it on, and waited for the water to get to the right temperature. Without looking back, he held out his hand and waited for her to place hers in his.

Ryan stepped to the side to allow Shannon to get wet. He placed her hands on the tile and entered her from behind. He thrust in and out, slow and steady, until they both came together. "How am I going to stand now?" Shannon said with smile.

"I'll take care of everything," was Ryan's only reply, even though his knees were weak. He would take care of Shannon, knowing she would take care of him, too.

They washed each other's hair and bodies and dried off. Shannon turned around to say something, before she heard Ryan's stomach growl even louder and started laughing again. "I guess you're hungry?"

"Why don't we get dressed and go downstairs to eat. I'll make us an omelet," Ryan suggested. *This is my chance to talk to her and get a feel about her staying with me.*

"Sounds goods. I'll help," Shannon told Ryan as she finished getting dressed.

The house lay quiet as they made their way into the kitchen. They both worked together without talking to get breakfast done. It was as if they had been together for years instead of days or weeks. They got everything out, started the coffee, and got the plates and utensils out without bumping into one another. Every so often, when one of them would get close enough they would touch an arm, or a waist to reach something on the other side. Ryan would lean over and kiss her temple when they worked side-by-side, getting breakfast completed.

Ryan didn't want to think about a couple of things. One, Shannon leaving in four days. Two, her true feelings for him. She had become important and he didn't want her to leave.

He was going ask her what her plans were. Today.

"Omelets are done. Are the bacon and toast ready?" Ryan asked.

"Yes. I'll grab the plates," Shannon replied. They decided to eat at the kitchen table and not in the dining room.

"What are your plans for today?" Ryan hoped nothing so he could have the day with her.

"I really should call my friends and see what's going on. I did come here with them to have a vacation." Ryan could tell she felt a little guilty about not spending time with them last night and then not making it to the cabin.

Ryan looked up at her. "I was thinking about taking the horses out again for a ride to the lake. We never did make it to the waterfall."

"I really do need to call my friends, Ryan." Shannon's voice was pleading.

Ryan leaned over, taking her hand into his. "I hoped that you and I could..." Then he heard someone coming into the front door.

"Ryan! Are you here?" This came from a voice he didn't want to hear in his home, especially today.

Ryan closed his eyes for a second then looked up. *Why is Vicky here? Carly.*

Ryan turned to Shannon, who had a questioning look on her face. He must have had a shocked look. "Your ex?"

"I'll be right back. Please wait right here." Before she could say anything, Ryan got up and headed to the front of the house. He stopped dead in his tracks at the sight in front of him.

TWELVE

When he came around the corner, he saw Vicky strolling toward him as if she had every right to be there. "What are you doing here?" Anger poured through him, boiling his blood and clouding his brain. Halfway through his question, all three of his kids came into the house. His boys looked just a shocked as he felt; however, Carly ducked her head.

"Don't look at me like that. Carly said she's using you and is worried and wanted me to come." *This from a woman who had serial boyfriends during their four years of separation?*

"You have got to be fucking kidding me! One, I don't say anything about who you date or have around. Two, it's none of your business or the three of you for that matter." Ryan looked at all of them. Turning to Carly, he practically yelled, "You have *no* right to

151

make a comment like that, young lady. You don't even know her. If you had a problem, you should've come to me, not your mother."

"Dad, Dustin and I were worried at first because Shannon is on vacation and didn't live here. I really do like her. But, I did *not* have anything to do with calling Mom," Colby said in a rush.

Ryan faced Dustin. "You have to admit that you got serious with Shannon fast, but I'm glad you're taking time away from the ranch and finally giving Colby and me more responsibility. I'm just not use to seeing you date."

"Well, I didn't date before. Not because I wanted to get back with your mother; I just didn't want the complication of having another woman in my life." Ryan tried to keep his anger under control and his voice low enough that Shannon wouldn't hear.

Stunned by his statement, his ex-wife said, "I resent that comment, Ryan. We had a good marriage, and I gave you three children."

"Our children have nothing to do with the reason we separated and got divorced, Vicky, and you fucking know that," Ryan stated firmly. "Carly, you had no damn right to call your mother and tell her anything about who and what I am or am not doing. It's none of her business."

Ryan needed to get everyone out. He worried that Shannon was going to show up any time now. He looked at his ex. "You need to leave and not worry about what I'm doing. Worry about yourself." Then he turned to his children. "The three of you can leave. I'll talk to you all later."

Everyone looked toward the kitchen, and Ryan had a very bad feeling. He whipped around to see Shannon standing there with a look of sadness on her face. Her purse was on her shoulder and cell phone in her hand.

"I called Lisa and asked her to pick me up. She should be here by now. I'm going outside." Shannon played with her cell phone. That's when they heard a car coming.

Ryan slowly moved over to Shannon and reached out for her hand. She pulled away from him and backed up like a rattlesnake prepared to strike her. He ran his fingers through his hair as he looked around. "Shannon, just give me a minute. Please."

She shook her head as she headed for the door, giving everyone a wide berth. When he took a step to stop her, she held up her hand. "I just need to leave, now. Plus, Lisa is here."

He watched Shannon walk out the door,

not wanting to make a scene in front of his family. *Damn it! What the hell just happened? Everything was going great. Last night, this morning, and eating breakfast together.*

He felt raw and needed to sit down and think. First, though… "Vicky, go back to your damn place in the city. Dustin, Colby, you have ranch chores you need to take care of. Carly…" He took a deep breath. "I just need some time alone. We'll all talk later."

Carly slowly stepped forward. "Dad, I'm sorry. Yes, I called Mom and told her that you're with some woman that I didn't like. I hoped that you and Mom would get back together. If she knew you are dating she would come home. Then I went over to Dustin and Colby last night. We talked and Colby made me see that the two of you will never get back together. I tried to call Mom back, but she didn't answer."

"Carly, you still can't think that." Ryan was surprised that came from Vicky.

Ryan looked at his daughter, still with anger in his voice, "How many times…?" He stopped when he saw the tears in her eyes. "Do you have to work today?" With a nod of her head, Ryan continued, "Why don't you let Mrs. Conway know that you won't be in today. We'll talk later."

"Why don't you go outside and talk to her? Maybe she hasn't left," Colby said in a low voice.

Dustin peered out the window. "She left. The woman driving that car looked like she wanted to drive right through the house." Dustin nodded toward the door. Dustin and Colby walked outside with another word.

Carly started to say something until her mom placed a hand on her shoulder. "Go call Mrs. Conway."

Vicky followed Ryan to the recliner and sat on the arm of the loveseat across from him. Taking a deep breath, she said, "Carly really didn't mean to hurt you or your lady friend. I think you're little hard on our daughter. As soon as everyone's emotions calm, you all need to talk. The kids are old enough to learn the reason we married and the reason for the divorce. Getting pregnant and not being married at this time isn't a crime. We tried to make it work, Ryan. But we just didn't love each other. Respect, yes. Friends, absolutely. But, love, no."

When he just sat there, she added, "I take it her name is Shannon? She's very pretty."

Ryan leaned his head back, closed his eyes, and prayed for patience. "Yes, her name is Shannon. I'm at a loss here. I talked to the kids and told... asked them to talk to me and not call you with what was bothering them. They didn't say much. Dustin and I had a slight argument. Where am I screwing up? I don't know what to do and have no idea how her two kids feel."

"You haven't screwed up, Ryan. There is nothing that can be done. I believe Colby is fine. But Dustin and Carly will have to work this out themselves. All you can do is what you're doing now. Talking and listening." Vicky's voice was sympatric.

Opening his eyes, he said, "I'm sorry to say this. Do you think I wouldn't be having these problems if you told them you and Pete are engaged?" This was the longest conversation that he'd had with Vicky in a long time. Messages were usually passed to and from their children.

Vicky looked guilty, "Maybe. How about..."

A knock on the front door stopped whatever else Vicky had to say. He jumped to answer the door in hope that Shannon came back. Carly beat him to it, though. "Hi, I'm here to see Shannon and Mr. Collin."

Ryan couldn't believe it was really happening. The man at the door had to be Shannon's son. He wore U.S. Army ACUs, with a nametag that had Shannon's last name, and tan boots. He had some of Shannon's features but must have more of his father's looks.

Ryan held out his hand. "You must be Dylan. I've heard a lot about you and your sister from your mom. I'm Ryan Collin and this is my daughter, Carly. Come on in. Did your mom know you were coming?" When he moved out of the way, he noticed his boys rushing up to the house from the stables.

"Thank you, sir. No, Mom didn't know. I wanted to surprise her." He looked around. Ryan knew he was looking for Shannon.

Ryan came in behind Dylan, and before he sat down he whispered to Vicky, "You need to leave right now, before this get any worse."

"I'll go. But for the record, I just came here to find out what the hell happened. Carly had been calling me. You're right, I need to tell them." Vicky looked sincere. "I really hope everything works out for you, Ryan. Talk to you later." With that, she left.

When Ryan turned around, Dylan had his arms crossed. "I called Bianca and she told me I could find Mom here. But Mom isn't here, is she?" Just then, his boys rushed in. *How can this day go from fantastic to totally screwed in just four hours? Fuck.*

"No, she already left. Can we sit down and talk?" Ryan hoped he could explain and just maybe get some advice from her son about how to get Shannon to listen.

With a nod, Dylan sat down in the recliner, followed by Ryan and all three of his children. The looks on their faces told him they didn't plan on leaving. Carly was almost in tears, clearly understanding that she'd played the largest role in what was going on. He was going to have to talk to his kids alone, and soon.

As he looked up at Dylan, his face was a mask that Ryan couldn't read. "First, these two are my sons…"

"Dustin and Colby. Yes, I know. Mom told me all about you, your kids, and this ranch. I talked to her about two days ago, and she seemed so happy. I haven't heard her this happy in a very long time, and I thank you for that. I even asked if she planned to move here. She said you two hadn't discussed anything about wanting her to stay. So, I asked for time off to come here and talk to her in person and to meet you. Plus, I needed to let her know that I'm getting deployed," Dylan explained with a straight face. *He must be mad or upset, and his military training has him controlling his emotions.*

Ryan wasn't sure how to start, and was stunned over what Dylan just said. "Well, everything is going great. I hoped to talk to Shannon this morning about her plans about staying. I didn't get that chance. The woman you saw a little while ago is my ex-wife. She came here because…. Well, let's just say that things got out of hand."

Ryan looked at Carly seated between her two brothers. She had her head down, her hands fisted in her lap.

"I don't know if I should listen to what you have to say, or leave and tell my mom never to talk to any of you again from the looks on everyone's faces. If my mom just walked out and left, then she got hurt. Plus, she did tell me that your kids were just 'okay' toward her. Not really sure what that meant." He said the word *kids* with anger, and he noticed his boys moving slightly, sitting at the edge of their chairs. "I think maybe I need to talk to my mom first."

As Dylan started to get up, Ryan tried to stop him. Carly replied before Ryan could say anything, only looking at her lap. "I wanted my parents back together. I called my mom and asked her to come here. What I didn't know was that Dad and your mom were together in the kitchen eating, and things got said. I made a mistake that I will forever regret. If you have to be mad at someone, I'm the one to blame, not my father." Everyone could hear the sadness in her voice and see the tears running freely down her face as she hugged herself.

Ryan hurried over to his daughter, took her hand, and pulled her off the couch. Hugging her close, he whispered above her head, "It's going to be okay. We'll work it out." He glanced at Dylan, who looked confused and unsure.

"Okay. Tell me what happened. Then I'll go see my mother." Dylan sat back down.

Breathing out in relief, Ryan let go of his daughter, took his seat, and proceeded to explain the morning's events, starting with breakfast. No way in hell was he going to start with when they woke up. He'd do whatever he had to if it meant he might get Shannon to stay with him. *This will work out. I love her. She's worth fighting for.*

Ryan was surprised that Dylan listened to everything he had to say, and his children, without interrupting. He knew he would have to let him know how he felt about his mother. He remembered that Shannon said he was the calmer one and would listen, analyze, and come up with a solution. He just hoped he would know what to do now, and would help.

When Ryan finished, Dylan asked, "Do you know how much she heard?"

"I wish I did, but I can't say for sure." Ryan rubbed his hands over his face.

Just then he heard Rosa. "Ryan, did you leave the dishes on the table? What did Shannon say about…?" She stopped when she turned after placing her purse on the foyer table. "Am I interrupting something?"

"Rosa, this is Shannon's son, Dylan. Dylan, this is my housekeeper, Rosa." Ryan and Dylan stood when Rosa came over to shake his hand.

"Oh, I've heard so much about you, young man, and your sister. Alexis, right? Your mother is very proud of your service to our county. Where is Shannon, anyway?" Rosa then turned from them and looked at his three children. With a scowl on her face, she scolded, "You three have a guilty look on your faces. Alright, get up and come with me to the kitchen and let your dad and Dylan talk."

Ryan noticed the three of them didn't move. Rose placed her hands on her hips. "I know you don't want me to have to repeat myself. Come on, move." With that, the three of them got up and went to the kitchen.

"She would make a great drill sergeant,"

Dylan said with a slight chuckle. "I wouldn't want to piss her off, that's for sure."

Ryan just smiled at him. "She does have everyone doing what she wants and when she wants it done. She knows things before I do, most of the time. Rosa and Hank, her husband and my foreman, are like family. So, about your mother..."

"Don't worry. This can be fixed, Mr. Collin. She doesn't like to feel like she's getting in between family or friends. So, she has a tendency of backing off. But if Lisa or Erica picked her up, they're plotting your death as we speak. Those two are the wild ones and have seen Mom unhappy and hurt. Especially Lisa. She took Mom to the hospital when my dad passed away. She doesn't want to see her like that again. I'll go and talk to her."

They both stood up and headed to the front door. "Thanks. Let me give you my cell number, so you can call me. And, please, call me 'Ryan'." He needed to let him know just how serious he was about Shannon. "Dylan, I want your mom to stay with me. This might seem fast to some, but I've never been so at peace and happy with any woman. That includes my ex-wife. I know you don't know me, but I would like your support and your sister's, too. I know what it would mean to Shannon."

"That's why I came. I wanted to talk to you and see if you're serious or just playing with my mom. I can tell you care about her just as much as she cares for you." They shook hands and Dylan left.

Ryan watched Dylan get into his SUV and drive off. His sons stopped to watch Dylan drive away then turned to look at him.

He didn't move at first, then turned and headed back into the house. *Now I have to wait and hope Dylan can help. Patience is not my strong suit. Okay, I'm not waiting… I'm driving over. After I get cleaned up.*

With that last thought, Ryan rushed upstairs to take a shower. It gave him the time he needed to think about Shannon and try to see things from her side. It didn't work. After his shower and shave, he went downstairs to get his keys. His sons turned to walk over to him until they realized he was leaving. They both stood there and watched him leave.

THIRTEEN

Sitting on the couch, Shannon had one leg under her while Lisa got drinks. "It's a little early to be drinking wine, Lisa." *Her answer to everything lately is to drink wine.*

"What is wrong with his damn kids? You are a great person and mother," Erica repeated to herself for the third time.

Shannon had the time to think about everything and felt calmer. She regretted leaving Ryan's house the way she did, and should've stayed to talked to Ryan and his children. But she didn't want to cause a fight between them. She could understand Carly wanting her parents together. No one would want their parents divorced.

Lisa sat down and, after handing out the glasses of wine, she and Erica started talking about ways to make Ryan pay. Bianca only asked who was in the house, which was damn weird. But, oh well. They all started talking about having to leave soon and not wanting to go back to work.

When Shannon heard a car pulling up to the cabin, she hoped it would be Ryan. But, when Bianca rushed to get the door and opened it, she was shocked to see her son, Dylan, coming through the door. "What are you doing here?" She got up to hug her son.

"I came here to see you. Got time off and drove here. I arrived early this morning." He fully entered the room and received hugs from everyone else. "You two causing trouble?" He had to laugh at the innocent looks on their faces.

Lisa and Erica had shocked looks on their faces. "Us? We're angels." Lisa said, batting her eyelashes as Erica sang, "Like a Prayer" by Madonna.

"Oh my God, Erica." Shannon turned to Bianca. "You knew about this. That's why you asked who was at Ryan's."

"Maybe," Bianca said with a small smile on her face.

"Mom, why don't we go outside?" Dylan looked at his mom and, with a nod, they headed out.

For a while, they didn't say anything as they moved to the back porch picnic table. *Oh boy, this is going to be good.*

"So…" She looked at her son, wanting him to start. "I didn't think you would really make it. Why didn't you say something? Considering we talked on the phone, what, about two days ago."

Dylan took a deep breath. "I came here to see you." When she only lifted an eyebrow at him, he finished. "Okay, to see you and meet this Ryan guy. Secondly, I'm being deployed and got the time off to see you before I leave. I wanted to make sure you didn't just turn your head, go home, and have regrets. You won't do anything when you get home."

"You're getting deployed? For how long?" Shannon never thought that would happen. Well, she hoped that it wouldn't happen.

"Is that all you heard?" Dylan said. "I just left Ryan's ranch, after I met him and his kids. I heard what happened. Want to talk about it?"

"No. Maybe." Shannon breathed out and crossed her arms on the picnic table. "How do you feel about me dating someone? Do you think I'm being unfaithful to your dad?"

Dylan looked stunned. "No, I don't think

you're being unfaithful, and I don't think Dad would want you to spend the rest of your life alone. You have enough love in your heart for Ryan, and I know you do or you wouldn't be upset over the fight. And, just so you know, Alexis feels the same. We already talked. She knows I'm here."

She was not sure if she should be talking to her son, but it did affect him and his sister. "How can I see him when his children want their parents back together? How am I going to leave here and not see him again? He's the first man I've dated who made me feel anything since your father. I loved him, but I want to share my life with someone. I don't want to be some old lady with twenty cats."

He started laughing at that last comment. "Cats. Really? Twenty cats?"

"Dylan, that's not funny." Shannon did her best not to chuckle by biting the inside of her mouth.

"Mom, yes, it is. I think you really need to go see Ryan and talk about everything. Dad, your kids, his kids and your…."

"Feelings we have for each other." That came from the one man she so wanted. *Ryan*. "I think I can take it from here. Thanks anyway."

Dylan reach for his mother's hands and squeezed. "Listen to each other and talk. Don't let this pass you by." With that, he got up to head back to the cabin. He stopped and put his hand on Ryan's shoulder. "Didn't want to wait for the phone call? Don't blame you. I wouldn't move if I wanted to work this out."

Ryan came around to sit in front of Shannon. He took her hands. "Shannon, please look at me. We need to talk."

Shannon glanced up at Ryan and saw all the sincerity and worry in his eyes. "What do you expect me to say? I won't come between you and your children. I don't want to be one of those girlfriends who's forever at odds with your family."

"I talked to my children and told them they're old enough to know better. Yes, Carly had no right to call her mother and try to get us back together. My sons just want me happy, and you make me happy. Vicky...well, she and I know it's over between us. We only got married because she got pregnant and it was the honorable thing to do. I wanted to be in their lives, so we tried to make it work. Instead, we made each other more miserable. We stayed together for the children in the beginning, and just never finished with the divorce until about three years ago." Ryan went on to explain everything. "We attended marriage counseling to try to make everything work. But, there was one thing always missing: We didn't love each other."

Ryan got up, going to Shannon to pull her to her feet. He leaned against the front of the table and tugged Shannon to stand between his legs. He needed her closer. "I want you to stay here with me in Montana. Make a new life here. You don't have to work, only if you want. Instead you can help me with the accounting books. I really hate the accounting end of the business. What do you say? Most important, how do you feel?"

Shannon didn't know what to say. She just looked at Ryan and wondered if she could really leave everything behind and take the risk to love again.

"Please, talk to me. What is going through that mind of yours?" Ryan worried that he would lose her before they even got a chance.

She placed both hands on his chest. "I want a life with you. But are you sure Dustin, Colby, and Carly can live with the fact that you and their mom are over? I won't come between you and your children, and I would never ask you to choose." She rested her forehead on Ryan's chest while his arms went around her and kissed the top of her head.

He whispered into her hair, "I love you, Shannon. We can go back and talk to them together. You can even bring Dylan and then we can call your daughter. Just stay here with me and make me the happiest I've ever been. We'll work everything out. I need you to trust in me; trust us."

"I do want to be with you. I haven't felt this alive in a very long time. But you have to understand I will always love Tom. We had a good marriage and raised two children. I won't forget him." Shannon had to make sure he understood. Tom would forever have a part of her.

"I don't expect you to forget or not still love him. I just hope you have enough love to add me to the list. We'll work on anything that comes our way, together." Ryan hoped he would get through.

Shannon just looked at Ryan for a few minutes. "Yes, I love you, too. I'll stay."

"How about we have a barbeque at the ranch for everyone? Both friends and family. You and I can head over now and talk to my children, along with Dylan." Ryan knew that this would work.

"Okay. That sounds like a plan. Why don't we go in and tell everyone?" Shannon pulled back, but Ryan reached for her and kissed her with all the passion and love he had.

After the kiss ended, Ryan just held Shannon tight in his arms and ran his hands up and down her back. *This is the first day of the rest of our lives.*

Ryan and Shannon walked back into the cabin and everyone froze. "Well, that didn't take long," Lisa stated.

"Okay, you two. I take it you're staying. Dylan just filled us in on everything that happened." Erica had a smirk on her face.

Ryan smiled wide. "Doesn't take me long to say I love you. I hoped that you three can come over for a barbeque. We're going to head over and work out some important issues with my kids." Turning to Dylan, he said, "We need you to come with us back to my place, if that's okay."

"This is going to be the beginning of many family gatherings." Dylan stepped over to his mom. "You good?"

Hugging her son, she said, "Yes, I am. You said you spoke to your sister. Is she really good with this?"

"I wouldn't have said so if she wasn't," Dylan replied.

Plans were made to meet up at the ranch, and Ryan called J.P., Steve, and Frank. He planned to call his sister and parents soon. Shannon rode over with Ryan while Dylan followed them.

* * *

Dustin and Colby had talked about what happened and needed to make amends with Shannon. Carly called in to work, still upset over what happened between her and her dad. She even talked to Rosa.

"Carly, you are not a little girl anymore. You need to understand that your parents being divorced is between them; the three of you are not added into the equation." Rose hugged Carly and rocked her back and forth.

Colby rushed into the house and found Carly and Rosa in the kitchen. "Dad's truck and another truck are coming down the driveway. I think it's Shannon's son." Then he rushed right back out.

Rosa looked at Carly. "Go on, girl, and meet your dad outside. Now."

"Thank you, Rosa. Love you." Then she rushed off.

* * *

When Ryan pulled up to the house, Dustin, Colby, and Carly waited in the front yard. Dylan parked his SUV next to Ryan's and got out. Looking to Shannon, Ryan took her hand.

"You ready?"

"I really don't know now. This all happened this morning and it's almost three. Maybe this isn't a good idea. Maybe we should wait until tomorrow."

Ryan wasn't sure how fast or hard he should push. Thank God Dylan opened the door. "Chickening out, Mom? Come on. If it gets too hard, I'll take you back to the cabin and Ryan can deal with them."

"Shannon, I want to get this all out. Please."

Shannon just leaned in and kissed Ryan on the cheek. "Okay."

As they headed up to the front door he stepped past his children, holding Shannon's hand has he walked into his home. Dylan followed right behind them and then his kids. Ryan went right into the family room and sat down with Shannon on the loveseat, and waited for everyone else.

For a while, they all just looked at one another. Then Rosa came in with a tray of glasses and iced tea. When she got up to leave, she mouthed to Ryan's children, "Say something." Straightening, Rosa glanced at Ryan and mouthed the same thing to him then left the room.

Ryan's children looked at one another. "To

be honest, I'm not sure what to say." Colby forever the spokesman of his children. He's also the one closest to Ryan.

Ryan could tell that Shannon was ready to bolt. It was Dylan who spoke first, leaning forward in the recliner. "So, are the three of you going to keep giving them shit or are you going to try to get along with my mom?"

"How are you taking this so well? This is your mom with my father. Aren't you worried about your father being replaced?" Dustin sounded curious.

"One, no one will ever replace my father. I don't think Ryan would even try to replace him and, if he tries, it won't work. Two, I don't want my mother being alone for the rest of her life. She's still young and has a long life ahead of her. I want to see a smile on her face, hear her laugh again, and I want her to love again. My sister and I just want her happy and, if Ryan makes her happy, that's good enough for us. However, if he hurts my mom, he will need to watch his back," Dylan stated. "Does that answer your stupid-ass question?"

Carly had her head down as she sat between her two brothers. "I'm sorry for what I did. I just never thought that my parents would really get divorced. I wanted them together. I didn't know you were here this morning. It won't happen again. Can we start over and get to know you? Please?" Her voice shook at the end.

With a sigh, Shannon looked up at Ryan then gazed at his son. "I don't want to replace your mom. I would never do that to you or your siblings. But I would like to be friends. I want to be with your father. But, like I told Ryan, I won't stay and be the reason for any discomfort within his family."

Ryan glanced at his children. "I've asked Shannon to move in with me. I've always told you three to follow your heart and to live your life to the fullest. Now, it's my turn. I'm not asking for your consent, but it would be nice to have your support and blessing."

Dustin started to say something when they heard a car drive up. It was too early for everyone to arrive yet. Ryan was a little disappointed that they wouldn't get their talk finished. Rosa came around. "I got it."

"Hi. I'm looking for Shannon and Dylan," came the second voice that Ryan didn't know. *Could this be Shannon's daughter, Alexis?*

She skipped into the family room with the biggest smile on her face. She said with excitement, "Mom! Dylan, I told you I would make it. You owe me twenty bucks, big brother."

Dylan got up from his seat with a shake of his head. "I said in the morning. You didn't make it this morning since it's almost evening, smart ass." He gave his sister a hug and kiss.

"I had to try. Can't believe you got here first." She hugged her brother with everything she had then rushed over to her mom and hugged her. "Hey, Mom. How are you? You must be Ryan. It's great to meet you." Alexis gave Ryan a hug that surprised him.

"Did the two of you plan this?"

"Well, that would be a big fat yes," Alexis stated with a smile on her face. Turning around, she said, "You must be Dustin, Carly, and Colby. I've heard about the three of you." She held out her hand to each of them. They shook her hand but didn't say anything. "Did I come in on something? Where are the ladies, Mom?"

"Here, sis, take my seat. You may want to be involved with this, too." Dylan seemed a little too happy with himself.

With a serious expression, she looked at everyone. "What the hell is going on? This doesn't look good."

"Let's just say some have... how to put this? Issues with Ryan dating our mother." By the smug look on Dylan's face, he knew what would happen.

Ryan noticed the dirty look that Shannon gave her son. "Now, this doesn't involve you two. So, just…"

"What, they have a problem with our mom? What the fuck is wrong with you three? Don't you want them to be happy?" Alexis was very upfront, Ryan thought to himself.

Dylan just sat back with a shit-eating grin. *That boy is happy with himself.* "Now, Alexis, we are working this out. Just sit there and be quiet." Alexis started to open her mouth, no doubt to make a smart-ass comment. "I mean it."

Ryan wasn't really happy. But he did have to respect the fact the Shannon's kids were upset on their behalf. "Okay, let's get it all out." He turned to his kids. "Your mom and I will *not* be getting back together, now or ever. I want Shannon to move here and be with me. All of you can respect the fact that we are grown adults, or you all can stay the fuck out of this and keep your damn mouths shut from here on out. You need to choose."

Dylan responded first. "Like I said, I'm good. As long as Mom is happy, I am."

"I'm not sure what the hell happened here, but I'm with my brother. Just don't hurt my mom, Ryan, or all hell will break loose," Alexis stated.

Ryan looked at his kids. "Well? I want all of you to be honest here." They all looked at one another and Colby started to talk. "No; Dustin, Carly, you two talk. Colby is not your voice." He looked at the son in question and they both smiled. Colby shook his head.

Dustin spoke first. "I'm fine with everything, Dad. Shannon, I'm sorry if I upset you in any way. It's just different, that's all. You're right, Dad. I owe you more than an apology for everything."

"I won't cause any more trouble. I talked to Rosa and my brothers and realized what I did was wrong and selfish. I only thought about myself. I'm sorry. I would like to get to know you and maybe be friends." Carly looked up for the first time, with hope in her eyes.

"That would be nice. We can go shopping and go for lunch." Shannon smiled wide.

"Rosa, you can come out now. And Hank, too." Ryan just knew they were listening.

Rose and Hank came around the corner. "I had to make sure everything went the way it should. Plus, I wanted to meet Alexis, too, so I don't feel guilty at all." Rosa headed right over to Alexis, who stood up with a smile and gave the woman a hug.

"I like you already," Alexis said with a huge grin on her face.

Rosa turned around. "This is my handsome husband, Hank. Hank, this is Dylan and Alexis."

"It's nice to meet you both. I take it everyone is coming over for a cookout?" Hank asked Ryan.

It always amused Ryan how not only Rosa, but Hank, too, knew what was going on without him saying anything. "Yes."

"Well, since I didn't get enough notice, I took out hamburgers and hot dogs for the grill. I just finished the salad and have beans heating up. Cake is in the oven and will be done in fifteen minutes, and we have ice cream in the freezer. Would you like anything else?" Rosa stated with satisfied look on her face.

Hank placed an arm around his wife. "No, that's great. What would any of us do without you?"

"None of you would get anything done, and don't you forget it, mister," Rosa said with a satisfied smirk and headed into the kitchen with Hank following behind her.

Dylan laughed. "I'm telling you. She would

make a damn good drill sergeant. No one would want to go up against her."

That seemed to break the ice in the room. Everyone either laughed or made a comment. The tension in the room lessened and the conversion turned to happier things. Dylan and Alexis talked about where they lived, what they did, and answered questions from Ryan and his children. Dustin and Colby talked about what they did on the ranch.

Shannon went up to her son and hugged him tight, and Ryan knew where the conversation was heading. "You said you're being deployed. When? Where to? How dangerous is it? Will we be able to talk to you?" Ryan could see and hear the tears in Shannon's voice, and his heart hurt for her.

"What?" Alexis grabbed her brother's arm.

Ryan spoke up, "Okay, everyone sit back down so Dylan can tell us."

"Yes, I'm being deployed. No, I can't tell you to where. Mom, don't ask, I'm under orders. Because you were so close to the base, my commander gave me leave. I will be able to contact you and will give you my overseas address as soon as I have it. I leave in one month and won't be home for six months. This is all I can say," he explained while kneeling in front of his mother and holding her hand.

Ryan put an arm around Shannon and could see the pain and how scared she was for her son. She wiped the tears from her cheeks and nodded her head. "Okay. I don't think I want to know too much anyway. It will only make it worse. Just write or call me. Alexis and I will write and send you care packages."

Ryan held out his hand to Dylan. "Anything you need, you let your mom, us, know. We'll get it to you."

They watched as his sister embrace her brother. "You watch your 'six' and come home safe. I love you."

Ryan noticed his kids coming over and shaking hands or fist bumping Dylan, letting him know that they would watch over Shannon and to be safe. It warmed his heart that everything was coming together. All the kids were talking about getting together before Dylan and Alexis had to leave.

During the conversation, Kim, Colby's girlfriend, showed up and introduced herself. Carly then talked about herself and how she wanted to attend college but didn't know what to take.

"You can always get the general classes out of the way," Alexis told her. Those two then started talking about college and courses.

"Ryan, I'll have to go back to Florida and give notice, and put my house up for sale and pack everything up. It will take about a month or two before I can get back here." Ryan knew it would take time, but didn't realize how long until Shannon mentioned it.

"I'll come with you and help," Ryan stated. He didn't want to be separated for that long.

Dustin had to remind him of a show he'd committed to attend. "I can go and get everything done for you, Dad." Colby jumped right in to help out, which didn't surprise him.

"You don't have to. I can hire some helpers." Shannon didn't want to put anyone out.

"Are you sure? Kim, you okay with Colby being away for about two to three weeks?" Ryan asked.

Kim looked at Colby first then shot a quick glance to Dustin. *Interesting…* "I needed to let Colby know tonight that Mom and Dad are going to see my aunt and uncle in Oregon and wanted me to go with them. So, I'll be away for about a month."

As the plans were being made, everyone started to show up. Shannon's friends were startled to see Alexis, but happy, too. Ryan's friends started showing up. JP got Stan to man

After Hours and he even brought his twin cousins, Max and Mitch. Frank and Nell showed up, with Steve right behind them. Everyone who meant something to him was there. Life just got better.

They all went outside to eat, talk, and tell some stories that made them all laugh. Ryan pulled Shannon into his lap and wrapped his arms around her. "I'm going to miss you while you're home," he whispered into her ear.

"I was thinking about that. I think I only have to give one week. I'm only going to send the things I really want and donate the rest. If my friends want anything, they can have it. The company I work for knows realtors I can list the house with and, when it sells, the closing documents can be mailed to me here," Shannon explained.

Ryan had a look of relief on his face. "So, that means you won't be gone for a month, but a week." At the look on her face, he corrected himself. "Okay, two weeks. I think I can handle that. I'm going to need to add the boys as authorized signers to the ranch. This wouldn't be happening if I did that already. I would be able to come with you."

Being so relaxed, they didn't realize how late it had gotten. The boys decided that Dylan would stay with them so they could get to know each other. Alexis and Carly headed back to the cabin with Shannon's friends. This gave Ryan and Shannon the house to themselves.

After everyone left, Ryan and Shannon went outside and cuddled together on the porch swing. He didn't know how long they sat there.

"Can you be happy here, Shannon? I mean, without being able to see your friends any time you want to?" Ryan wanted to make sure she would have no regrets.

Shannon sat up and straddled Ryan, placing her hands on his face. "You have made me feel alive. I never thought I would find love again, but I have. I'll see my friends. They can come here and visit me. Plus, between us we have five kids to keep us busy. I love you, Ryan."

"And I love you, too," Ryan replied and leaned in to kiss Shannon with everything he had, putting all his feeling into that one kiss.

FOURTEEN

The next three days went by fast. Everyone got together as much as they could. Shannon stayed at Ryan's every night. During the day, she spent time with her friends and her children. Carly spent time with Shannon when she didn't work at the bookstore. Shannon even picked her up for lunch and they walked around town to spend some time together.

Shannon helped Ryan with getting everything together for his trip. They were leaving on the same day. He packed his duffel bag and got all his paperwork for his meeting with the Farm and Ranch Association. His attorney was working on getting his sons added as signers to everything regarding the ranch.

Colby's girlfriend, Kim, left the following day, so he had time to get packing done. Ryan purchased a plane ticket for Colby on the same flight with Shannon.

The day came that Shannon had to leave to head home. She hadn't told Ryan, but she'd already contacted her boss both by phone and email, letting him know that she handed in her notice. Shannon didn't want to be away any longer than necessary. Ryan's meeting would only last a week, tops. Maybe ten days.

"So, I'll see you in two weeks," Ryan said as he held onto Shannon. He bent down and kissed her forehead.

Shannon reached up. "It will go by fast. We'll both be so busy that time will fly. I'll call you every night."

With that, Ryan said goodbye to his children then got into his truck and drove away.

"Okay, Colby, you ready to head out?"

* * *

Shannon and Colby worked morning to evening to get everything done—putting the house up for sale, deciding what she wanted, what to send to Dylan and Alexis, and what to donate. Her boss let her leave without completing her one-week notice. Shannon decided not to let Ryan know so she could surprise him by being at the ranch before he got home.

"Shannon, I just finished the....oh, I'm sorry I didn't know that Bianca was here." Colby looked down at the little three-year-old girl hugging her mother's legs. She was the cutest blonde-haired, blue-eyed little girl he had ever seen.

Shannon turned around. "Hey, Colby. I'm trying to convince Bianca to come back to Montana with us. She just lost her job and needs a change."

"That would be great. I know Dad wouldn't mind. You should call him." Colby sat down next to Mia, who finally sat down on the floor to play with her stuffed animals. He loved kids and noticed that Mia was just as shy and quiet as her mother.

"Okay. I'll do it, but I'll have to leave when my brother and sister-in-law are at work. And, since I don't have much, I can fit it all in my Malibu. Do you have four boxes I can have?" Bianca looked at Shannon with hope in her eyes.

Shannon watched Colby play with Mia. "You're really good with her, Colby." Mia looked up and smiled, and signed, *I like him*.

Colby looked to Mia to Shannon, "What did she say? I don't know American Sign

Language." Colby handed Mia the stuffed teddy bear.

"She said she likes you." After Shannon told him, he looked embarrassed.

"I'll go put the boxes in your car for you, Bianca," Colby offered. "I'll be right back, Mia. Okay?"

After Bianca and Mia left, Shannon and Colby got ready to head back to Montana. She couldn't wait to see Ryan. The moving company got the last of Shannon's things to either go to Montana or her children. What was left in the house, Lisa and Erica would donate for her. They were also going to look after the house until it sold. Erica's car broke down, so she bought Shannon's. Colby found a small box that had hidden compartments that he wanted to give to Kim. Shannon let him have the box to give to his girlfriend.

Shannon and Colby got to the house one day ahead of Ryan. She unpacked the boxes that had already arrived. Some were her clothes and others items that meant something to her: pictures, jewelry, and odds and ends.

"Hey, when did you and Colby get here?" Carly leaned against the doorframe.

Shannon got up from the floor and made

her way over to Carly. "Last night late. Come on in." Shannon and Carly were still working on getting closer. "I have something for you."

"Really?" She could hear the excitement in her voice.

"Yes. Oh, where is it? Here, this is for you." Shannon handed Carly a small ceramic box with blue flowers on top. As she opened it, she took out a gold necklace with an emerald and six diamonds.

She just looked at Shannon with tears in her eyes, and the emotion that showed her how much this gift meant to her. "I can't accept this. It's too much. You should be giving this to your daughter, not me."

She could tell how much she really wanted the necklace. "Yes, you can. My daughter has one just like it. I got them when my late husband and I went to Ireland. I'm giving mine to my step- daughter... well, hopefully one day. I called Dylan and Alexis and they're fine with me giving this to you. Alexis even said the two of you can wear them at the same time when she comes to visit."

Carly hugged Shannon tightly. "Thank you. I love it and will cherish it always."

They both worked together, opening the rest of the boxes and finding places to put everything. They talked and laughed and had a great time. "Oh, I almost forgot; Dad called me to check in. He's coming home tonight around dinner. I can make myself scarce so you two can have dinner together."

With a smile Shannon replied, "That would be great, but only if it's okay with you. How about all of you come over here in the morning and we can have breakfast together as a family? That's one thing I missed when my kids moved."

"Okay. Well, I gotta go to work. I'm going to let Dustin and Colby know what's going on and that I'll be staying with them tonight." Carly got up and hugged Shannon before she left.

Shannon got excited about Ryan coming home tonight. She rushed and got everything put away, cleaned the bedroom and bathroom, and replaced the sheets. *Tonight is going to be special.*

One of the boxes held candles that she'd bought in a scent called Midsummer's Eve. She placed them in the bedroom and the Ocean Mist in the bathroom. She took a shower and took her time shaving her legs and her mound completely bare. Under the navy blue sundress, she wore a sheer mesh and lace teddy.

She came downstairs to start dinner and found that Rosa had already fixed dinner. "Now, don't you get upset. You're running out of time, so I got everything done for you. Steak, mashed potatoes, gravy, and broccoli... his favorite. The dining room table is set for two, including candlesticks, and I got a bottle of red wine from the refrigerator. All you need to do is relax and keep everything on low heat. I'll see you for breakfast." Rosa kissed her cheek and went to Hank, who stood at the back door.

"Thank you, Rosa."

About thirty minutes later, Ryan's truck pulled up to the house. She started the radio—country music, of course—and waited by the table.

* * *

Ryan was tired and hungry. He just wanted to eat, shower, and call Shannon. God, he'd missed her. Being away from her made him realize that he didn't want to be away from her ever again. He couldn't wait for her to come home.

He got out of his car and looked at the barn, wondering if he should check on the horses. Maybe after he ate. Walking up to the house, he heard the radio. Why would Rosa leave the damn thing on? "Rosa?" he called out, with no answer. Again, "Rosa?"

He started to head upstairs when he noticed the light in from the dining room. As he turned the corner, he stopped dead in his tracks. "Shannon." She looked absolutely beautiful in that sundress with her hair half up on the sides. The table was set for two, with candles and wine. He dropped his duffel bag and walked over to the woman who held his heart. "What's all this? When did you get home? I talked to you this morning, and you said you would be home in a few days."

She reached out and took off his Stetson, and placed it on the other end of the table. "I didn't want you to know that I got in yesterday late. This is all for you. Surprise!" Taking his hand, she squeezed. "Go wash up, dinner is done." Ryan's heart swelled and he leaned over to kiss her. She pulled away. "Go. I'm hungry, and I don't want dinner to get cold or burn."

After Ryan washed up in the downstairs bathroom, he went back into the dining room and Shannon had the plates and wine ready. They ate and talked about their trips.

"I called my boss and emailed him before I left to go home. He let me leave without working the week out, so we had a lot more time to pack up and put the house up for sale.

Bianca lost her job and needed a change, so I invited her to come to Montana and stay with us, just until she found a place to live. I hope that's okay with you.

"That's fine, Shannon. They're both welcome. Max and Mitch will be glad to see her. Don't look at me like that. They are interested in her and, yes, I told them she has a daughter. But let's not talk about them, okay?"

As Ryan finished eating he told her about his trip. "I'm getting two more horses. They will be here in about two weeks. Someone abandoned a farm, so the group of us are taking in all the animals. The boys will have to get ready for them."

They cleaned up the table and placed the dishes in the dishwasher. A knock on the door startled them. Ryan looked at Shannon. "I'll get it." As he moved down the hall, his sons came through the door. "Hey, boys. Is there a problem?"

"No. Just wanted to say 'night to Shannon, and realized you were home," Dustin replied.

Colby gave his dad a one-armed hug. "We'll talk to the two of you in the morning at breakfast. Night, Dad. Come on, Dustin."

"Shannon?" Ryan called out. *Where the hell*

did she go?

She answered, "I'm upstairs."

Ryan went and grabbed his duffel bag and headed upstairs. When he got to his bedroom door he froze in place and dropped his bag, again. Candles flickered in different places in the bedroom, giving the room a romantic glow. Shannon stood by the nightstand, in a silk robe that stopped just above her knee. She must have brought up the wine and glasses. He slowly moved over to her and could smell the shea butter on her. "What's all this?"

"Why don't you go take a shower first." Shannon took Ryan's hand and walked him into the bathroom. More candles were lit in there. Unlike the bedroom, they smelled like the ocean and coconuts. She had everything laid out and, when he turned, she ran the water in the shower. *Okay, I'm going to go along with this and find out what exactly she has planned.*

Ryan took the fastest shower that he could remember ever taking and wrapped the towel around his waist. While he dried off, Shannon went back to the bedroom and closed the door behind her. He shaved, brushed his teeth and, with one last glance, he headed into the bedroom only to be stunned again at the sight before him.

Dear God! Damn! Shannon stood by the bed with her long hair down and the robe gone. He could now see what she'd had underneath the dress. She wore a sheer mesh and lace teddy with openings for her breasts — her very exposed breasts. Ryan shifted over to her and stopped a foot from her. With one hand, he cupped her cheek. "You're full of surprises. You are breathtaking. If this is what happens when I go away for a week, I might have to go away again. I love this. When did you plan all this?"

He ran his fingers down her neck, over her collarbone and down her breast, stopping right above her nipple. He raised an eyebrow to her, waiting for her to answer. "I, um, got this at a store before I left. And you don't get to go away without me," Shannon panted out.

Before she finished speaking Ryan started drawing circles around her nipple, but not touching it yet. He wanted her wild and mindless. Bringing both hands up to cup her breasts, he squeezed them lightly. Then he started to glide his hands lower under her breast to her ribs and her hips. Shannon raised her hand up toward Ryan. "Put your hands behind your back, Shannon. I want to explore this teddy a little bit more. If you touch me, it will be over way too soon."

She slowly lowered her arms and placed

them behind her. "I need you to touch me."

"Oh, I will be soon. Be patient, baby." He turned to sit on the edge of the bed, keeping the towel around his hips. Ryan leaned forward and turned Shannon by her hips so she stood in front of him. His hands traveled around to cup and squeeze her ass. "Move forward, Shannon, and straddle my knee but don't sit down."

She did as he asked. Keeping a hand on her ass, he eased his right hand down her ass to her thigh and up to her pussy. While his hand roamed downward, he finally took one of her nipples into his mouth and sucked hard. Ryan cupped her sex and moved his palm, then froze for the third time. He released her nipple with a pop and looked up at her to see a blush color her cheeks and neck.

"What's this? An open crotch, too?" He slid two fingers inside of her. "Already wet and shaved." He pumped his fingers in and out in a slow and steady rhythm.

Shannon moaned loudly. "It's a surprise. Ryan, I need to come. I can't last much longer."

"I know. All I have to do is touch this hard bud that's peeking out and begging for attention to know." As Ryan stated what he wanted, he placed his thumb on her clit and rubbed it in circles. Shannon dug her nails into his shoulders as she came. "That's it, Shannon, come for me." He curled his finger to rub her g-spot, and she went over the edge again. He loved the lust on her face. Gorgeous.

Shannon fell forward into Ryan's arms. Her hand went to the towel and pulled until it released. Going to her knees, she licked him from base to tip. "Shannon, stop. I won't last if you keep doing that."

"Isn't that the point?" she replied with a wicked smile.

"I want to be inside you." She stood up and started to remove that teddy. "No, leave it on."

Pushing herself up to her feet, Ryan cupped both breasts and took one nipple into his mouth. Then he moved to the other nipple while one hand moved to her ass. Releasing her breast, he nipped at her mouth before kissing her deeply. Turning her around, he stood and she crawled up onto the bed and Ryan climbed up over her.

"I can't wait anymore, baby. I need you too badly." With that, he reached down and guided his cock to her entrance and thrusted. And stilled. *Shit, I forgot a condom.* "Baby, you feel so damn good. But, I have to tell you I don't have a condom on. Please, I want to stay bare. I'm clean."

Shannon looked at him with lust-filled eyes. "So am I. Please move. I need to come again."

Ryan moved inside her. He had never felt this way toward someone. She tightened around his cock, and he almost lost complete control. "You feel unbelievable. So damn tight." He went to his knees and placed her leg on his shoulder and got deeper, his eyes going crossed from the feeling. Shannon moaned and he knew she would go over the cliff of pleasure soon.

"Not yet, baby. Together, and I'm not ready to let go."

"I can't, Ryan." Shannon's legs tightened and she started to shake as she used the leverage to be able to move.

Ryan froze deep inside her. "Yes." She tried to move, but Ryan wouldn't let her. Shannon then froze when she felt a finger at her ass. "Be still." Ryan slowly pushed the tip of his finger into her and waited. He did this three more times until his finger was totally inside.

"Ryan, please move. I can't... can't wait." Shannon having a hard time expressing herself in the firestorm of passion and need overtaking her.

He started to move his cock in and out of her pussy in time with the finger in her ass. He reached out with the other hand and squeezed her breast, pinching her nipple. He felt his balls tighten painfully and knew he was a goner. He moved faster, needing to come now himself. "Now, baby. Come with me now."

As soon as the words left his mouth, both of them came with shouts. He looked down into her blue eyes, still filled with all passion and emotion. He pulled out of her slowly and gathered her into his arms and held her tight. With a chuckle, he ordered, "Don't you fall asleep. I'm not done with you yet." Shannon just turned to face him and smiled as she cuddled into him.

"I love you. You're the best thing that has happened to me in a very long time. I'm glad my friends talked me into this vacation." Looking into her face, he could see all the love in her eyes. "When Tom died, I didn't want to feel that pain again. I built a shield around my heart until I saw you at the diner and felt the crack. I never thought I would find love again. But I did, with you, and this ranch."

He placed a kiss on her forehead and breathed in that delicious scent that was Shannon. "After everything that happened with my ex, I closed my heart, too. Seeing you, I had to talk to you, get to know you and just be close to you. Your eyes drew me to you. Never did I believe that I would say to anyone that I loved them. But, you changed everything. I'm living again and loving again. I love you, baby."

He rolled Shannon to her back and slid inside of her for the second time that night. *I'm going to make love to her slowly and passionately. Being inside her is coming home.*

Life with Shannon is going to be heaven on earth. He could see their lives together, working on a ranch, with his sons by his side, and coming into the house to the woman he loved and who loved this ranch just as much as he did. Ryan felt blessed and fortunate.

EPILOGUE

Eight months later

Bianca sat at the front table with her daughter, Mia, while they watched Shannon and Ryan speak their vows. Shannon looked stunning in her light blue dress, and Ryan wore dress pants with a fancy western shirt and his Stetson. She wondered if he ever took his Stetson off. In fact, looking around, every man there wore a Stetson.

Shannon's son, Dylan, gave his mom away and, boy, didn't he look handsome in his dress uniform. Her daughter, Alexis, and Ryan's daughter, Carly, stood next to Shannon. Ryan had his sons with him. Mia was the flower girl and looked adorable in her pale pink dress. Bianca was overjoyed for Shannon and Ryan. Both of them looked so content. So why was she depressed and wanting to run off and cry? *Because this is what I should've had with Scott.*

She moved out of Shannon and Ryan's house and into an apartment in town. Frank even hired her at the diner and didn't mind Mia coming to work with her. She loved to go to the diner and help show everyone to their tables and hand them menus. When Mia needed a nap, she would go into the little office Frank had in the back and sleep on the loveseat he had. Frank and Nell loved having her around, and acted like her aunt and uncle.

Scott was the problem. Bianca feared him and what he was capable of doing. He had a violent temper and wanted everything his way…or else. He didn't want Bianca from the moment she'd gotten pregnant. He even went as far as to blame her for the pregnancy. His mother had found out about Mia, and now demanded Scott to get full custody. She wouldn't lose her child.

So Bianca ran to Montana. Her brother and sister-in-law didn't even know where she'd gone. She only left a note saying why she left—not telling them where—and that she would be in touch. It took Bianca almost two months to call her brother and, when she did, he was frantic to know what happened, where she was and why. Scott was looking for her now, after all this time. Bianca only would tell him what was going on, but not where to find her. Only that she was okay and safe and would call him back next month. Well, it had been four months and she still hadn't found the courage to call her own brother back. She missed him so much. After the death of their parents, they only had each other.

Problem number two came in twos: the twins, Max and Mitch. Who were now looking at her, and not Shannon and Ryan. Bianca was so busy thinking of everything else, she didn't notice her daughter now sitting on Max's lap. They played with her stuffed black bear that they got for her. Mia loved the bear and took it everywhere with her. God, even her own daughter was fascinated with them.

The wedding and reception were being held at *After Hours*. Shannon's friends had one table and Ryan's friends had a separate table.

Shannon and Ryan got to Bianca, and she gave them both a hug. "Both of you look great. It was beautiful. Congratulations to you both!"

Both of them said at the same time, "Thank you."

Shannon leaned in to whisper into Bianca's ear, "Looks like Mia found two handsome cowboys. But I bet they're also interested in her mother. You think?"

"Shannon!"

"Just saying. Go for it, Bianca. I want you as happy as I am." Shannon hugged her friend, and Ryan guided her over to Lisa next.

When she turned, Max and Mitch stood in front of her. "I believe I have someone who is hungry. I'm not sure what she's allowed to have." Max looked from Mia to her as he bounced Mia in those massive arms.

Mitch placed a hand on her upper arm. "We'll have to change that. We need to know what she can have and if she is allergic to anything." She must have had a surprised look on her face. "Don't look at me like that. This will happen, Bianca. We want you and Mia. What are you so afraid of?"

That was the problem. She wanted them just as badly. But Scott would find her, and then what? *Oh, I am in sooooo much trouble.*

The End

Don't miss a release announcement

Join Christa's mailing list:

http://eepurl.com/ce7prI

ABOUT THE AUTHOR

Christa Ann started out writing poems like her mother. One day, stories started coming to the front of her mind. Romance, shifter, western, and places unknown, but they demanded to be created. Her debut novel, *Finding Love Again* — a contemporary western romance and first in a tantalizing new series — releases in the fall of 2016.

She grew up in Maryland and now lives in Southwest Florida with her husband, daughter, and two kitties (one Bengal named Jasmine, and one Maine Coon named Midnight.) She's also a proud military mom. Her son is currently serving his country.

Some of her favorite things are being with her family and friends, reading, hiking, traveling, and her love for chocolate. Being Irish/Scottish, Christa also Irish step dances with her daughter and loves St. Patrick's Day and Bunratty Mead. She also enjoys playing her piano… she's been playing for 36 years.

Follow Christa on social media:

Website: http://authorchristaann.com/

Facebook:
https://www.facebook.com/profile.php?id=
100011364957108&fref=ts

Twitter: https://twitter.com/Christaann10/

Email: AuthorChristaAnn@gmail.com

Sign up for news and updates:
http://eepurl.com/ce7prI

If you enjoyed the book, please consider leaving a review, even if it's only a line or two; it would make all the difference and would be very much appreciated.

Thank you,

After Glows Publishing

Follow After Glows on social media

Website: https://afterglowspublishing.com/

Newsletter: http://eepurl.com/bOB8v1

Facebook: https://www.facebook.com/AfterGlowsPress/

Twitter: https://twitter.com/afterglowspub